DAUGHTER OF THE AMAZON

Borgo Press Books by JOHN RUSSELL FEARN

1,000-Year Voyage: A Science Fiction Novel * *Anjani the Mighty: A Lost Race Novel* (Anjani #2) * *Black Maria, M.A.: A Classic Crime Novel* (Black Maria #1) * *A Casebook for Brutus Lloyd* * *The Crimson Rambler: A Crime Novel* * *Don't Touch Me: A Crime Novel* * *Dynasty of the Small: Classic Science Fiction Stories* * *The Empty Coffins: A Mystery of Horror* * *The Fourth Door: A Mystery Novel* * *From Afar: A Science Fiction Mystery* * *Fugitive of Time: A Classic Science Fiction Novel* * *The G-Bomb: A Science Fiction Novel* * *The Genial Dinosaur* (Herbert the Dinosaur #2) * *The Gold of Akada: A Jungle Adventure Novel* (Anjani #1) * *Here and Now: A Science Fiction Novel* * *Into the Unknown: A Science Fiction Tale* * *Last Conflict: Classic Science Fiction Stories* * *Legacy from Sirius: A Classic Science Fiction Novel* * *The Man from Hell: Classic Science Fiction Stories* * *The Man Who Was Not: A Crime Novel* * *Manton's World: A Classic Science Fiction Novel* * *Moon Magic: A Novel of Romance* (as Elizabeth Rutland) * *The Murdered Schoolgirl: A Classic Crime Novel* (Black Maria #2) * *One Remained Seated: A Classic Crime Novel* (Black Maria #3) * *One Way Out: A Crime Novel* (with Philip Harbottle) * *Pattern of Murder: A Classic Crime Novel* * *Reflected Glory: A Dr. Castle Classic Crime Novel* * *Robbery Without Violence: Two Science Fiction Crime Stories* * *Rule of the Brains: Classic Science Fiction Stories* * *Shattering Glass: A Crime Novel* * *The Silvered Cage: A Scientific Murder Mystery* * *Slaves of Ijax: A Science Fiction Novel* * *Something from Mercury: Classic Science Fiction Stories* * *The Space Warp: A Science Fiction Novel* * *A Thing of the Past* (Herbert the Dinosaur #1) * *Thy Arm Alone: A Classic Crime Novel* (Black Maria #4) * *The Time Trap: A Science Fiction Novel* * *Vision Sinister: A Scientific Detective Thriller* * *Voice of the Conqueror: A Classic Science Fiction Novel* * *What Happened to Hammond? A Scientific Mystery* * *Within That Room!: A Classic Crime Novel*

THE GOLDEN AMAZON SAGA

1. *World Beneath Ice* * 2. *Lord of Atlantis* * 3. *Triangle of Power* * 4. *The Amethyst City* * 5. *Daughter of the Amazon* * 6. *Quorne Returns* * 7. *The Central Intelligence* * 8. *The Cosmic Crusaders* * 9. *Parasite Planet* * 10. *World Out of Step* * 11. *The Shadow People* * 12. *Kingpin Planet* * 13. *World in Reverse* * 14. *Dwellers in Darkness* * 15. *World in Duplicate* * 16. *Lords of Creation* * 17. *Duel with Colossus* * 18. *Standstill Planet* * 19. *Ghost World* * 20. *Earth Divided* * 21. *Chameleon Planet* (with Philip Harbottle)

DAUGHTER OF THE AMAZON

THE GOLDEN AMAZON SAGA, BOOK FIVE

JOHN RUSSELL FEARN

Edited by Philip Harbottle

THE BORGO PRESS

MMXIII

DAUGHTER OF THE AMAZON

FIRST BORGO PRESS EDITION

Published by Wildside Press LLC

www.wildsidebooks.com

DEDICATION

For John Robert Colombo

CONTENTS

THE GOLDEN AMAZON
by Philip Harbottle

In 1943 British writer John Russell Fearn decided to quit writing for the American pulp science fiction magazines, and to concentrate instead on books for the English market. Within a very few years he became established as a leading novelist in several genres, not only science fiction, but also mystery and detective fiction, and westerns.

His first new SF novel, *The Golden Amazon*, was published by World's Work in April 1944. In this story, a little girl of three years of age is made the subject of an idealistic scientist's illegal glandular experiments. The scientist's dream is to end world wars by creating a woman devoid of the usual lusts and frailties of mankind, who upon reaching maturity would institute a benign scientific rule. But the apparently successful experiment has a flaw: it instills into the girl a hatred for all men, and a ruthless cruelty. Her supernatural scientific gifts enable her to master atomic power, and practically leads her to destroy the world. She breaks the will and strength of men, and elevates women to positions of wealth and power. She also discovers human synthesis, and by this means she is able to escape retribution when she is eventually overthrown. She is seen to collapse and die, a victim of consuming ketabolism, echoing the memorable finale of Rider Haggard's *She*. In actuality, it was only her synthetic image, and this paved the way for the *Golden Amazon Returns*, and further sequels

Fearn sold reprint rights in the first novel to the prestigious Canadian magazine, the Toronto *Star Weekly*. The magazine carried a special Comics Supplement, the center section of which was a 'complete novel', published in newspaper format. Aimed at a general readership, the novels were written by the top popular novelists of the day, including John Dickson Carr, Ellery Queen, and P. G. Wodehouse. They sold hundreds of thousands of copies, and the novels were syndicated to several American newspapers in the Maine and New York areas. The Amazon novels enjoyed extraordinary popularity (especially with Canadian housewives), and ran for the next sixteen years following the appearance of the first novel in the March 3, 1945 issue, ending with Fearn's sudden death in September 1960, aged only fifty-two. His final two Amazon novels appeared posthumously.

During Fearn's lifetime, only the first six novels were published in British hardcover editions from the World's Work in England, after appearing in the *Star Weekly*. This was because the publishers discontinued their entire fiction line in 1954. However, the Amazon novels continued to appear in the *Star Weekly*, eventually notching up twenty-four titles.

Fearn had resold paperback rights to the Canadian publisher Harlequin Books, but after publishing only the first three titles, they stopped publishing SF and other genre fiction to concentrate on their famous Romances line.

Meanwhile, as early as 1949, Fearn had realized that the Amazon series had the potential to run indefinitely. This presented him with a problem, however. The 'origin story' of the Golden Amazon was conceived and actually set during the Second World War. Subsequent novels were written during the war and the immediate postwar period, and projected their stories only a few decades into the future.

He very astutely realized that to keep ahead of reality, he needed to move the Amazon *further* into the future—first into the outer solar system, and thence to the stars. So with the seventh novel, he introduced a new main character, Abna of Atlantis—someone as equally intelligent, and even stronger than herself. These dynamics provided him with an *interstellar* canvas, thus ensuring that the series would remain ahead of reality.

Fearn's strategy was a great success, and the Amazon novels retained their popularity, ending only with his tragically early death in 1960. By then he had written a further twenty Amazon novels, and made preliminary notes for his next (which would later be written by Fearn's biographer, Philip Harbottle).

Long after Fearn's death, his entire Amazon series

would eventually see print from the pioneering US small press Gryphon Books in limited paperback editions, and later by the Canadian Battered Silicon Dispatch Box small press in their hardcover Omnibus series.

This new Borgo Press paperback series will be the first trade edition of all twenty-one of these later novels by Fearn, beginning with the seventh novel in the original series. First published in 1949 as *Conquest of the Amazon*, I have edited it slightly as *World Beneath Ice* (The Golden Amazon Saga, Book One) so that it can be read and enjoyed by new readers who may be totally unfamiliar with what had gone before. Subsequent novels have also been slightly edited for modern readers.

The publishers hope that this new series may create many more "fans of the Amazon." Meanwhile, any reader interested in seeking out the earlier six Golden Amazon novels will find that they are readily available on the internet, and in numerous earlier paperback and hardcover editions.

* * * * * * * * *

To date, readers can enjoy the following new Borgo Press editions:

Book One: *World Beneath Ice*

In destroying the threat of an alien invasion, the Golden Amazon had inadvertently caused a decline in the sun's heat, encasing Earth in an ice sheet that threatens to eliminate humanity. The Amazon encounters Abna, a descendant of Atlantis, stronger and even more scientifically advanced than she, and the ruler of an Atlantean colony still surviving in a protected environment on Jupiter. She refuses his offer of marriage, but agrees to form an alliance in order to restore the sun and save the Earth. One thing that Abna has not told the Amazon is that all the females of his race have been wiped out by a bacilli infection....

Book Two: *Lord of Atlantis*

A gigantic ridge of land rises from the Atlantic floor, causing massive tidal waves on either side of the ocean. Even stranger, both England and America are then assailed by an invasion of prehistoric monsters! A gigantic domed city rests on the newly risen plateau, whilst out in space an alien spacecraft orbits the Earth. Such are the mysteries and challenges facing the Golden Amazon, self-appointed governess of Earth, as she struggles to unravel the maze of mystery that was the deadly legacy of Atlantis!

Book Three: *Triangle of Power*

The marriage of Violet Ray Brant—better known as The Golden Amazon—and Abna of Atlantis should have ushered in an era of peace and scientific prosperity to the people of Earth. But an unexpected turn of events finds Abna betrayed and marooned on a satellite

of Jupiter, and the Amazon flung far beyond the Solar System. With Earth's two protectors removed, the
planet is now at the mercy of another Atlantean, the
master scientist Sefnor Quorne....

Book Four: *The Amethyst City*

The metaphysical union of the Amazon and Abna
results in the mental creation of a fully mature daughter—Viona. Quorne, still struggling for domination,
forces Viona into a marriage ceremony, and impreg-
nates her. But with the intervention of Tarnec Brodix,
a super-mind from an external universe, Quorne and
Viona are separately flung into an ultra-dimensional
limbo. Abna chooses to follow after his daughter, leaving the Amazon to brood over the disaster, alone in the
Amethyst City of Saturn.

CHAPTER ONE
UNHAPPY AMAZON

Amid the poisonous wastes of the planet Saturn there lay one particular territory forever sacrosanct— an area of indeterminate size and completely apart from the atmosphere of ammoniated-hydrogen and plains of pulverized rock lighted by the twilight glow of a far distant sun.

In this territory were green fields and silver streams, the blue of an Earth summer sky, the gold of a warm sun, and in the midst of it an incredible city of amethyst-tinted metal. That a woman living here could not be happy seemed impossible,

Yet the Golden Amazon was the most unhappy woman in the System.

Hexa, the one servant who attended to all her wants, was secretly worried. So much so he finally put his thoughts into words as he came upon the Amazon lost in thought in one of the mighty lounges. He hesitated for a moment as he studied her—the most perfect woman ever born, the glare of the synthetic sun etching out every detail of her flawless figure in its close-fitting golden gown. Ageless beauty, superhuman strength, scientific genius. All these attributes, but the Golden Amazon was desolate.

"May—may I speak with you, Amazon?" Hexa asked at last.

The Amazon glanced up in surprise. Hexa moved forward, a muscular young giant in a Grecian-type toga.

"Certainly, Hexa. What is it?"

"I have been noticing, Amazon, how distraught you are. I wondered if I could do anything to help?"

"I'm afraid not, Hexa—though I appreciate your asking. You know the situation as well as I do. My husband and daughter have gone—forever, as far as I know. My daughter is in the Twenty-Fifth Plane of matter, and my husband also. And my daughter's husband is in the Twenty-Seventh Plane...."

"One can bring them back here," Hexa ventured.

"I know—but I do not wish it." The Amazon turned to look at the servant directly. There was a tiredness about her deep violet eyes. "If you had the choice of recovering your daughter and your sworn enemy, what would you do? I cannot have my daughter back without her husband because they are in the same mathematical matrix."

"I should be inclined to risk the enemy," Hexa answered,

The Amazon shook her head. Hexa was not acquainted with the scientific ruthlessness of Sefner Quorne, husband of Viona, the Amazon's daughter. Once back in the normal plane he would, once again, set no limits on his ambition.

"I think," the Amazon said presently, "that I am making the mistake of staying in surroundings which constantly remind me of my husband and daughter. It was in this city of Millennia where it all happened. Instead of it bringing the peaceful pursuit of scientific problems, as my husband had intended, it has brought me only grief."

Hexa did not answer. He was thinking of Tarnec Brodix, the Mind of Minds, the super-mathematician of an exterior universe who could, with his astounding computations, restore Viona, Abna, and Sefner Quorne at any moment he was asked. But the Amazon still set her face rigidly against it,

"I shall return to Earth," she decided finally. "There may be problems there requiring my attention."

Her decision made, it was typical of her that she wasted no time in putting it into effect. Within an hour she was in her spaceship, the *Ultra*, pulling away from Saturn's vast surface into the void.

She brought the mighty machine down at the main London spaceport and it attracted no particular attention since the populace in general was conversant with the comings and goings of the strange woman who—though not officially—ruled the entire solar system.

Her first call was at the executive office of the Space Line. Chris Wilson, head of the Earth-end of the line, looked up in surprise as the Amazon came into his office. He glanced briefly over her black-suited form with the scarlet cape at her shoulders, then rose with extended hand.

"Hello, Vi. Been ages since I last saw you. People have been asking where you've been."

"Have they?" the Amazon said indifferently.

She settled in a chair, and Chris looked in puzzled interest at the distance in the girl's unfathomable eyes and the droop about her usually resolute mouth.

"Been far?" he asked.

"Saturn. I have lost Viona forever. And Abna. I am utterly alone! It began when Tarnec Brodix, the master mathematician, disrupted Sefner Quorne into the 27th Dimension," the Amazon explained. "Since Quorne is married to Viona, the mathematical configurations also affected her. You will remember how she became transparent, and finally disappeared. She vanished into the 25th Dimension, two stages removed from her husband because, although mated, they are not identical in molecular makeup. I asked Brodix to bring Viona back, but that he cannot do without bringing Quorne as well. I refused to take that risk. Abna and I quarrelled over it, and finally he decided to go and stay beside Viona and protect her. Brodix arranged that. That left me alone."

"Your only answer to that, Vi, is to have Brodix bring Viona and Abna back and take your chance on Quorne."

The Amazon shook her head. "I dare not, Chris. He has only one avowed intention—to destroy me, and Abna, if he can, and rule the System. When I last saw Viona, some months ago now, she was going to have a child. It will be hers and Sefner Quorne's. Thus has he perpetuated himself. What that child will be like I shudder to think, unless it has inherited more of the characteristics of Viona than Quorne. That is another reason why I dare not bring even Viona back. I have only one satisfaction—Quorne is probably the most unhappy man in the Universe because there is withheld from him one mathematical factor in his makeup. That will make him an eternal victim to an unsatisfied longing. The torture of incompleteness will always be upon him. That missing factor is in the mind of Tarnec Brodix."

Chris said: "I cannot see why with your tremendous knowledge you cannot have Brodix bring back all three and then deal with Quorne."

"And alienate Viona? Whilst both Abna and I know him to be a scientific force for evil, Viona is young and sees Quorne only as a misguided scientist who is, nonetheless, likable enough otherwise. She has never realized his real depths. If I were to wipe him out, she would never forgive me."

"You've lost her anyway. Why not take the risk and let Brodix get busy?"

"No. Quorne is one man of whom I am really afraid. He has knowledge that even exceeds mine in many things.... No, I shall let things rest and hope that memory will slowly die and leave me as I was to start with—a lone wolf, caring nothing for anybody. With a woman like me sentiment should have no place, and yet it has. The surgical operation that made me a superwoman was not complete. It left me with emotions, and I cannot always rule them."

A clerk came in with a message, and the Amazon rose.

"Anything needing my immediate attention?" she asked. "If nothing is required, I'll retire to my Surrey home and lose myself in experiments. I had better get used to being alone again."

"No, nothing," Chris said. "The world is at peace and everybody seems more or less satisfied. Conditions are normal on Mars and the Moon and—" Chris stopped, looking at the message in his hand. "Take a look at this," he said.

The Amazon took the note handed to her. It was on the Space Line communication form and read:

"Have space pilots check up on unexplained dark patch in remoter deeps of space. Not clearly visible from Earth and would bear investigation. Office of the Astronomers."

The Amazon read the message and for a moment there was something of the old gleam of interest in her eyes, then it faded out.

"Probably a dark area like Cygnus," she said, handing the message back. "They appear at times.... Well, since there is nothing more exciting than that I'll be on my way."

Half an hour later she was in her own home in Surrey—a home of scientific gadgets and robot servants, yet with a touch of femininity here and there. The Amazon had a meal, changed into laboratory coveralls, and then considered what to do next. At the back of her mind was the memory of the message Chris had received. She could not help her scientific interest even though she had brushed the matter aside at the time. In another hour it would be nightfall....

"Better than nothing," she muttered to herself and went into the laboratory-observatory annexed to the house. By the time she had adjusted the light-wave telescope to her satisfaction, an instrument infinitely more powerful than any other in the world since it drew light-waves unto itself in their original clarity from any given distance, the darkness was deepening and the night was clear.

CHAPTER TWO
SUPER-SCIENTIFIC RESEARCH

A switch opened the roof and she settled in the scanning chair and peered through the eyepiece. An adjustment of the focussing screw brought the hosts of heaven leaping into relief, a picture such as she might have seen anywhere in space except that in this case the atmosphere prevented the pin-sharp brilliance existing in the void.

She searched far out to the remote spaces in the region of the North Star, searching out beyond Orion, the Coal-Sack, and the Black Hole of Cygnus.

Then she saw it—a roughly-formed circle of utter darkness in which not a single star or nebula gleamed. Beneath her fingers a switch clicked and the nearer-focus control came into operation. Immediately the stars on the edge of the darkness vanished. In all her experience she had never seen anything quite so black. There was not the faintest trace of radiating streaks, not even the ghost of nebulous dust. And the one thought hammering in her mind was that it had no conceivable right to be there.

Getting to her feet, she switched on the observatory

lights, and going to the filing cabinet, she pressed a button. A series of slides, illuminated from the back, paraded before her vision—photographs of the cosmos, which she had made in her sell-imposed task of photographing the entire known Universe.

When she came to plate sixteen she removed it from its rack and studied it carefully. It showed exactly the same portion of heavens at which she had just been looking. It had been originally photographed a year ago and at that time the stars were numerous. Now there was only the Darkness, as yet only a smudge on the face of infinity, but one day—

She crossed to the radio-phone and switched it through to the observatory at Mount Wilson, California.

"Violet Ray Brant here," she said as a voice responded. "What do you make of the queer dark patch in section eight of the Northern Hemisphere?"

"I'm glad you brought up the matter, Miss Brant," the official in charge answered. "I was thinking of contacting you about it. All spaceport executives have been asked to have their pilots make a check on the phenomenon. Not that I expect much, since even if they travelled out as far as Pluto—which they don't— it would not bring them measurably any nearer this queer smudge."

"When did it commence to be seen?" the Amazon asked.

"About a week ago. It was only a speck at first, blotting out two stars. Since then it has grown considerably. When we take into account our distance from it, I am pretty well shocked when I think how big it must be. And since it is growing, it is obviously coming nearer."

The Amazon said: "Thank you for your information. I'll see what I can discover and let you know."

She returned to the telescope and for a while she gazed through it. Then she went to a bank of instruments and switches on an apparatus that, as the thermopile can measure heat from the surface of the Moon, gave a reading of distant space. The apparatus incorporated special fourth-dimensional processes, so that the outflowing detector-wave from the instrument was able to hurdle the void at speeds many times in excess of the speed of light.

Now and again the needle jolted and registered maximum in heat as the nearer stars were reached—then it dropped again to the zero reading of space. Hours passed. The distance must be stupendous. Still the Amazon waited, but to her amazement it was five-and-a-half hours before she got the reaction she wanted. The readings were at zero in every direction. Heat, light, electromagnetic energy—none of these things registered.

Her readings complete, the Amazon made a note of each one and then went back into the house to study them. She settled down and worked through the night, hardly stirring until 7:30 the following morning. Then she picked up the visiphone. The face of Chris Wilson, speaking from his home, appeared in the scanning-plate.

"Oh, hello, Vi! I was just leaving for work—"

"Chris, I've made a most disturbing discovery," the Amazon interrupted him. "You recall that message you showed me about a dark smudge in space?"

"Why, of course. But you said—"

"Since then I've looked into it, and my conclusion is that unless I can work out something in the meantime, the whole Universe is going to be blotted out!'"

"What!" Chris exclaimed. "Blotted out? How do you mean? Destroyed?"

"No. That would be merciful. Something much worse. Matter will remain, but light and heat and all forms of radiation will become things of the past."

"I don't understand, Vi."

"Come to my place right away," she said. "I want to show you what I've discovered."

"I'll come immediately."

The Amazon summoned one of her telepathic-responsive robots. It laid a meal and tidied the room. By the time Chris had arrived, he found the Amazon had changed into a sweeping gown instead of her coveralls, looking what she was—a superbly beautiful woman.

"Sorry to drag you from your work," she apologized, as they settled down and the robot attended to the refreshment, "but as the head of the Space Line, as far as Earth is concerned, you should know the facts. I am not going to broadcast them to the world as yet. Time enough to do that if my efforts to find a way round the difficulty should fail."

"Fail?" Chris repeated, surprised. "I never knew you

to admit such a possibility before. You, who created a sun when our own was destroyed; you who can destroy matter and build it up again—"

"Chris, no menace or difficulty I have fought before equals this one. There exists in the depths of space—inconceivably far away as yet—an ever-growing patch of non-space-time."

"What is that?" Chris asked. "Space is space, isn't it, no matter how you look at it?"

"Space is a loose term, Chris. The early scientists used to think that space was actually a medium in which radiation in all its forms could move. Without ether-of-space, as Eddington called it, there would be a total vacuum with no power to transmit radiation. It used to be thought that because of ether we see the stars by their light-waves, we feel the heat of the sun as his radiations are carried to us, and we hear radio, all because of the ether medium. Modern science subsequently showed that electromagnetic waves did not require any ether medium for their propagation. But they *do* require what we might call the fabric of space-time itself. Destroy *that* and we are alone indeed."

"You mean it can be destroyed?"

"I mean," the Amazon answered grimly, "that it *is* being destroyed. That is the meaning of that Smudge—as I will call it—out in infinity. How it came into being I don't know, but I do know that it is growing rapidly, expanding like an explosion, and at a speed greater than light itself. As it travels, all light and heat ceases. Stars which have been engulfed in it are giving no light or heat."

"Maybe they've been destroyed?"

"No. The mass detectors, which operate by displacement of bulk, show they are still there."

There was silence for a moment, and it was an uncomfortable one as far as Chris was concerned. Many a time in the past when a particular danger had threatened, he had discussed it first with the superwoman, just as he was doing now, but he had always found her confident of mastering the situation. It was a disturbing change to find her brows notched in uneasy thought and the coffee forgotten at her side.

"It may go away as strangely as it was born," Chris suggested, but the Amazon shook her head.

"Things born in space do not go away like that, Chris. They grow. In the end, if space-time itself is wiped out, it will mean that all the hosts of the universe will exist in a silent, utterly cold tomb in which no light waves, no heat waves—nothing can ever move. Can you imagine Earth like that? Absolute extinction of life because it cannot see or keep warm. That is what it amounts to."

"How long will it take to get here—this Dark?"

"As yet I haven't worked it out. I can do so in thirty minutes on the computer."

They went into the observatory, and while the Amazon worked with the mathematical instruments Chris looked at a film recording the Amazon had made the previous night. He saw for himself the awe-inspiring sight of an island of night amidst the blaze of the stars.

"Three years—maybe more," the Amazon said finally. "It all depends whether its faster-than-light acceleration continues to increase exponentially, or whether it reaches an optimum speed and remains constant. If its present acceleration is maintained, then three years will see Earth blacked out—and to try and escape it by flying to other worlds will not do any good, since they too will succumb until all the universe is dark and dead."

"But Vi, a thing as gigantic as this couldn't just happen. It upsets all known laws."

The Amazon was silent for a moment or two, then at length she made up her mind.

"I'm going to take a look at that Dark at close quarters," she said. "Telescopically I cannot sum it up. Its distance is so colossal that even though I travelled at the speed of light, I'd be several years reaching it."

"Then how can you reach it?"

"I will use my dissembly transportation method— dissemble my body and recreate it in space near enough to the Dark to study it. My prototype apparatus was limited to the speed of light, but since then I have modified it to operate through the fourth dimension. By that means I can foreshorten space and transmit myself many times faster than light if need be."

Chris shrugged. "You're talking way above my head, Vi. I shall have to leave it to you. Just let me know what you discover, and if there is anything I can do to help...."

"Hardly." the Amazon said, smiling drily. "If this problem taxes even me, haw do you hope to grapple with it?"

Chris did not respond. It was not the first time the Amazon had made him realize that compared to her, his brain was only equal to that of a new-born infant.

CHAPTER THREE
EVEN THE AMAZON IS BAFFLED

After Chris had departed, the Amazon spent two hours sleeping and then, refreshed, she went calmly about the task of preparing for her gigantic journey. She made her arrangements with the methodical precision of the true scientist. First she drew on a spacesuit, complete to the helmet—since she would resolve in the void itself at the end of her journey—and to it she fastened all the instruments she was likely to need. They included a brain-vibration telewriter, which, responding to her thoughts, would write down whatever notes she wished to make.

This done, she set the dissembling equipment beam to the required distance as given on the computer, and then she threw in the time switch and stepped onto the transmission plate. Presently the moment of dissolution came and, though she was steeled to it from previous experience, it was again an exquisite anguish as every atom of her being was broken down into its energy equivalent—including the spacesuit—and hurled through hyperspace at an incredible velocity.

During the transition the Amazon herself was as

completely lost to consciousness as one under powerful anaesthetic. The sense of returning life brought her to opening her eyes and she looked through the transparent visor of her helmet. She was suspended in empty space, just as she had calculated, so far from the nearest appreciable gravity field that she could not drift towards it. She was utterly motionless and would remain so until the apparatus on faraway Earth reversed its action and snatched her back whence she had come.

She turned her head slowly. There, no more than a few billion miles away, was the awesome barrier of the Dark. At such relatively close quarters it was terrifying, seeming to be sweeping inward like a titanic shadow and blotting out nebulae and stardust in its advance. The more she looked at it, the more the Amazon realized she might even be enveloped within it if the apparatus did not react exactly to the second she had calculated.

She pressed the button on her breastplate, which actuated the various instruments strapped to the outside of her suit. Each one in its respective way registered some particular aspect of the mystery, then via her telewriter she gave her own mental reactions to the Dark. And it came nearer, and nearer still. She watched distant stars winking out of existence before the advancing tide, as a lamp might vanish before clouds of smoke.

As she waited, the Amazon was filled for a moment with the consciousness of her own utter insignificance—and audacity. By her own skill she had projected herself to this point in space to gaze upon a mighty cosmic change corning over the face of things, and at the speed it was moving she might pay for it with her life. Still she waited, in ever-growing alarm, and saw the wall of night pouring down on her in a relentless tide. To judge its distance was impossible, as impossible as trying to measure the thickness of a huge shadow.

Then came that moment of unendurable tension and everything snapped out of existence. The next thing she knew the Amazon was struggling to her feet under the apparatus in her laboratory, her spacesuit still about her. Breathing hard, she dragged it off and stepped clear of the transmission plate.

Restorative tablets revived her sufficiently for her to continue working, and for the next two hours she was busy with the instruments on which, stopwatch fashion, she had taken her readings. Three hours later, she had come to an end of her calculations.

She called Chris Wilson—this time at the Space executive building, and he came quickly. Her first words shocked him.

"I'm beaten, Chris. Completely! This isn't just darkness. It's a complete flaw in the mathematical makeup of the Universe. The entire Universe is one flawless equation, perfectly balanced. Mathematics have vibrations, and if a vibration came from somewhere which upset the balance by a fraction, the entire Universe would change. That, I think, is what has happened. And the effect is seen in the cancellation of space-time as a known factor. I am not a super-mathematician, Chris, though I am a scientist. I cannot hope to grapple with a thing like this."

"There's one who can," Chris said. "Tarnec Brodix, or whatever you call him. You told me he was the greatest mind you had ever encountered."

The Amazon gave a wan smile. "You know, Chris, I have been so intent on trying to work this thing out, I'd forgotten all about him."

"What puzzles me is, how do you contact Brodix? He's in a Universe outside our own, isn't he? Inhabiting a planet made up entirely of mathematical postulations?"

"True, but he is sensitive to thought-waves. He came to my aid before when I concentrated—my thoughts winging the gulf to him at almost instantaneous speed—so there is no reason why he should not do so again."

"Instantaneous speed?" Chris puzzled, as the Amazon settled herself in a chair to begin concentrating.

"Certainly. Thought, Chris, is the swiftest messenger in the universe and untrammelled by physical laws."

With that the Amazon closed her eyes and concentrated. But seconds crept into minutes and nothing happened. The Amazon opened her eyes and sat motionless, waiting for some sign of that pale mist that would announce the arrival of the queer gnome-like being whose knowledge was beyond all human ken. Ten minutes passed. Fifteen. Then half an hour had gone.

The Amazon sat frowning. Then she said: "I have it!" She got to her feet. "The Dark is between Brodix and me, and that Dark will not carry any radiation, not even thought-waves. I'm utterly cut off from him."

"Then...what happens?"

The Amazon did not answer, but when she presently raised her eyes again and found Chris looking at, her she felt as though somehow he could read her thoughts. The fact seemed confirmed when he said simply,

"Abna."

"Yes, Abna might be able to overcome the trouble. He understands many things that I do not—and vice-versa. But that is no answer to the problem because only Brodix can ever bring Abna back."

"Without Brodix you're utterly lost, then?"

The Amazon did not admit the fact openly, but her expression was sufficient.

"I never thought it would one day come to this," Chris muttered. "That the Golden Amazon should find herself with a problem she couldn't solve, and be cut off from those who might help her. The people, when they eventually hear of it, will lose a lot of confidence in you, Vi."

"I can't help it, can I?" the Amazon demanded angrily, her violet eyes glowing. "I have far-reaching knowledge, and know it—but there are limits, and I've reached them. I—"

She paused and snatched up the visi-phone as it buzzed.

"Yes? Miss Brant speaking.... Mr. Wilson? Yes, he's here."

Chris took the instrument. "This is Wilson," he said, and listened attentively. The Amazon took little heed of him, lost in her own thoughts, until something in the tone of his voice made her glance up.

"And it has no insignia at all? From the direction of the outer planets? Yes, allow it to land in the usual way and have the spaceport controller make full inquiry."

Chris switched off and said: "A fairly large space machine has been reported heading for Earth. It does not belong to any of the known space lines. No contact has been attempted with it so far."

"From the direction of the outer planets, didn't you say?"

"Yes."

The Amazon motioned Chris to follow her. They went into the observatory and by the actuation of various switches the girl closed the roof except the trap through which the telescope projected. In consequence the observatory itself was thrown into total darkness. After a moment a glimmer of light came into being. The Amazon moved another switch and a screen glided into position where the scanning chair usually stood.

There was a click. Despite the daylight outside the light-wave trap in the instrument functioned perfectly and upon the screen appeared a vision of space. It changed rapidly as the Amazon spun wheels or played her fingers up and down a series of numbered keys.

Chris exclaimed abruptly, "There it is!"

The Amazon was already aware of the fact. She studied the screen intently. Clearly visible was a space machine totally unlike any used on the normal routes.

"That vessel is similar to the ones Abna used to have on Jupiter," she said. "For all I know, they might still be on Jove since it was partly resurrected."

The Amazon began moving swiftly. She switched off the instrument, restored the daylight, and then hurried into the house with Chris behind her.

"Where now?" he inquired, as the Amazon fled toward her bedroom.

"I'm going to the spaceport to meet that ship when it comes in. You can take me down in your car."

CHAPTER FOUR
SON-IN-LAW TROUBLE

At the spaceport she gave orders that the unknown machine was not to be interfered with in any way and that it was to be allowed a free landing—then she spent her time wandering about the building, keeping herself alert for the loudspeakers announcing the vessel's arrival. Finally the advice came through. Immediately she hurried out of the building and stood watching the machine come in.

Finally it settled. Obeying the girl's orders, no mechanics hurried to the machine. It was left to itself. The Amazon crossed the broad space to where the machine stood, keeping her eyes on the airlock. She realized that her imagination was probably running riot, that what she expected would happen was decidedly unlikely— Then her thoughts stopped and she came to a halt in her advance. The airlock had opened and a figure was standing there, gigantically tall and broad shouldered, blond-headed, attired in the semi-Grecian style of a high dignitary of Atlantis.

"Abna!" the Amazon whispered, going forward again and staring at him fixedly. "Abna! Then my guess was right!"

"Hello, Vi." He came forward, moving with his well-remembered dignity. But he was not smiling. His handsome face was cold, uncompromising. When he finally reached the Amazon he did not stoop to kiss her. Instead he looked at her intently.

"How did you get back?" she asked, recovering herself.

"From the Twenty-Fifth Plane? I don't know. It just happened."

"But it couldn't—"

"I tell you it did! I didn't ask to be sent back. I didn't even want it. Viona and I were making out quite well— She's with me."

"She is?" The Amazon swung away and hurried to the vessel's huge airlock just as Viona appeared in it. She was lightly clad, her copper-gold hair sweeping to her shoulders. But, like Abna, she was not smiling. Her sapphire blue eyes had a hard, staring light and the usual upturned corners of her mouth were dragged down. She looked bitter, resentful.

"Hello," was all she said, as the Amazon embraced her.

"What's the matter with you?" the Amazon demanded. "You and your father both look alike— disgruntled, embittered. Whatever differences we may have had we can surely meet again with a smile, can't we?"

Viona did not respond. Instead she glanced behind her into the roomy control cabin. The Amazon looked also. Standing by the switchboard was a familiar figure—hatchet-faced, with the forehead of an intellectual, his heliotrope-colored eyes full of sardonic amusement.

"Quorne!" the Amazon exclaimed.

"It has been quite some time since we met, Amazon," he commented, moving forward. "Possibly I am the cause of my wife and Abna looking so dispirited. They believe—or at least Viona does—that you intend to carry out your threat to destroy me now chance has brought me back again."

"Kill my husband if you dare!" Viona breathed, her young face venomous. "I won't stand for it, mother! I'm warning you! Sefner may be your enemy, but he's my husband—and I still love him."

"Bless the girl." Quorne murmured, smiling. "You see how much faith she has in me, Amazon? Be a shame to spoil her young dream, wouldn't it?"

The Amazon clenched her fists, her expression showing the mental struggle she was undergoing.

"This situation is one we cannot discuss here," she said. "I think it might be better to go to my home and talk it over. There is so much to be explained—"

"This control room is every bit as private as your home, Amazon," Quorne told her. "Viona—come inside and sit down. Tell your father the Amazon wants to clear up a few points."

Viona hesitated, then looked outside and called to Abna. After a moment or two he entered the control room and remained by the door, massive arms folded, a troubled look on his handsome face. Only Sefner Quorne seemed at his ease, lounging in an upholstered chair.

"None of us know how we came back from the dimensions in which we were lost," he said. "It happened abruptly. For myself, I was alone in the twenty-seventh matter plane, where I had been ever since that mathematical meddler, Brodix, hurled me. Then, without warning, I was on Saturn in the city of Millennia. Beside me were Abna and my wife."

"Correct," Abna confirmed, catching the Amazon's glance.

"And the baby?" the Amazon asked. "Did it come with you? Was it born?"

"It was not only born," Viona answered, "but the child is now two years of age—"

"But it isn't two years since—"

"Time," Viona interrupted, "passes much more quickly in those planes. The child is alive. It came back with me to the normal world. At the moment he is asleep in one of the rear cabins of this machine."

Quorne added: "I think it was the child who restored us to normal."

Already completely bewildered, the Amazon could only gaze in amazement. Quorne did not explain any further, but Abna did.

"Something happened to the child quite suddenly," he said. "Viona and I had made the best of life in the Twenty-Fifth Plane, finding it pretty much the same as the normal world with endless supplies of natural food, but no living beings. The child behaved quite normally for the two years following his birth, then he seemed seized with something that I can only call a fit of profound concentration. You never saw such a look on the face of a two-year-old child. Viona and I could only stare at him—and as we did so our surroundings clouded, changed position, and we were back in Millennia."

"And so was I," Quorne added. "And at that moment, for the first time since my transportation from things normal, I felt satisfied with life. A strange inexplicable longing which had constantly possessed me in the other plane was gone."

"Brodix withheld you from completeness by retaining a factor in your makeup," the Amazon told him. "The riddle is how you got it back again—how all of you came to be returned to normal. Naturally, the idea of a two-year-old child being responsible is ridiculous."

Quorne said: "Sefian—as we have called the child—has inherited my scientific tendencies and those of Viona, which she in turn inherited from you. He—"

"On the surface," Abna broke in, "he is a perfectly normal child. It was only on this one occasion when he behaved so strangely."

"I would like to see him," the Amazon said, rising. "Or maybe you object. Viona?"

Viona did not answer, but there was a sullen look about her mouth. The Amazon ignored it and followed Abna into one of the compartments. She moved to where the child was lying, and as Abna had said, there was nothing abnormal apparent. Sefian was a black-haired youngster with a high forehead, rudiments of a very straight nose, and cheeks with dimples.

"Vi," Abna said quietly, as the Amazon turned to leave again, "before you go I'd like a word."

"Very well."

Abna moved forward, towering above the Amazon as she eyed him coldly.

"For the sake of Viona, Vi, leave Quorne alone," Abna entreated. "Something unexplained has brought us all together again, so let it rest at that. I know Quorne was once your sworn enemy, but—"

"He is still my enemy, Abna. He will, if he can, destroy both you and me in an effort to achieve ruler-ship of the entire solar system. He has never had any other idea in his mind. However," the Amazon continued, "I shall not be openly hostile towards him because it would not serve my purpose at the moment. Galling though it is, I need him—and you."

"In what sense do you need me?" Abna asked.

"The scientific sense. I am trying to forget our union because we cannot agree as to what is right for Viona. But come back into the control room and I'll try and explain."

Abna nodded and followed the Amazon down the corridor. In the control room Viona was lounging against the panels. Quorne was still in the chair.

"The child's eyes, Amazon," he commented, "are identical with yours—violet. I am not sure whether I approve of that. I would have preferred the more purple tint of my own and—"

"We can forget the child for the moment," the Amazon said curtly. "There are more important things to discuss. I do not suppose any of you are aware that the Solar System has only about three to five years of existence left?"

Both Abna and Quorne gave a start, both of them knowing that the Amazon would not make such a statement idly.

"Why, what is threatening?" Abna asked, puzzled.

"Didn't you see it—a smudge of darkness on the remoter deeps? I thought you might have on your journey to Earth."

"We were too busy watching Earth to look behind," Quorne replied. "After our mysterious emergence on Saturn, Abna decided we should come to Earth in the only machine Millennia possessed."

"The Earth," the Amazon said, "is threatened by total darkness and cold. I've made every investigation and by myself I cannot defeat the trouble. I believe Tarnec Brodix could, but I cannot contact him through this Dark area. But I believe that our united intellects might achieve what Brodix could do singly."

The Amazon explained in detail, and the knowledge of the common danger threatening—though as yet so far away—did a good deal to break down tension.

Here was something with which they could all get to grips without human antagonisms coming in between. Quorne, first and foremost a scientist no matter what his personal ambitions, was immediately plunged into thought.

"If, as you think, this cosmic fault is mathematical," Abna commented, "then our united powers will be of no avail. Remember, I tried once before to master a similar problem."

Quorne observed, getting to his feet: "We have only the Amazon's own theory. She may be wrong."

"About the flaw being mathematical?" The Amazon's eyes were bright with challenge. "I am not wrong. I never am in things scientific."

"Nonetheless, I would like to think the problem out for myself. You and Abna do as you choose. Viona and I have our own lives to live and—"

"Just a minute," the Amazon snapped. "Does this mean you are not going to join Abna and me in trying to overcome this danger which is threatening?"

"I see no reason why I should. Abna has amazing powers, and so have you. I scarcely see that I could add anything." Quorne glanced towards Viona. "Fetch the child," he ordered, and without a word the girl obeyed.

"Apparently you have turned Viona into your servant as well as your wife," the Amazon commented.

Quorne smiled coldly. "I have seen what a woman can do if she be given her head. Meaning your illustrious self, Amazon. I do not intend her daughter to have any such chance."

"Meaning that our enmity is as complete as ever?"

"Meaning, Amazon, that now I have returned to Earth and can spare the time for thought, I shall devote all the power I possess to destroying the throne you occupy. And I believe I can do it. In many ways my knowledge transcends yours."

"You have overlooked that I will be fighting on the side of my wife," Abna said, his face grim.

"No." Quorne shook his head. "I am prepared for a struggle, and I shall win it."

"But what of this menace which is—"

"That is several years in the future. By that time I shall be master of the system and will then devote my energy to solving the problem of this—this Something coming out of space."

At that moment Viona returned, the child in her arms. The Amazon gave her a steady look.

"My place is with my husband," Viona said. "And I still see no reason why you should regard him as your enemy."

"You didn't hear what he said a moment ago," the Amazon answered.

Quorne moved his head briefly and, completely obedient, Viona pulled open the airlock with her free hand and stepped outside. Quorne glanced back over his shoulder.

"Where we shall settle I do not know," he said. "I have no wish to start fighting you any sooner than is necessary, Amazon."

Then he was gone, leaving the Amazon with her lips tight. Abna gave her a troubled glance.

"I notice it all the time Quorne is with Viona," he said. "He holds her in complete subjection, which, considering the force of his mind, isn't surprising. Whilst she was with me in the Twenty-Fifth Plane she was as normal as could be, considering the strangeness of our surroundings."

"She must go her own way," the Amazon said. "We have both Quorne and this spatial menace to fight. We had better get home, and think things out."

CHAPTER FIVE
VIONA VERSUS THE ZANJI

It was nearly midnight when the Amazon and Abna came to the end of every possible mathematical theory they could devise to counteract the onrushing enigma from space—but they were compelled to admit themselves beaten. The Amazon had come to the same dead end as before, and Abna was little better. Though he could, when necessary, make matter obey his will and possessed powers almost godlike in certain circumstances, he was now facing something utterly intangible. Literally nothing.

"As you said earlier, Vi, Brodix is the only one who can sort this out," he commented, throwing down his notes in disgust.

"I wonder," the Amazon said, "whether it would be worth the risk to fly around the Dark in an effort to find Brodix—as we once did when we expanded from this Universe into the next."

Abna shook his head. "The Dark would probably engulf us. I think we should leave the problem alone."

"Alone! But we can't, Abna! We can't!"

"I think we can. There is somebody else besides

Brodix who can master this business—our grandchild, Sefian."

The Amazon sighed. "Abna, be reasonable! The Dark could be here in three years, which will make Sefian five years of age. How do you suppose—?"

"When he is five in years, he will be completely mature. He does not evolve like a normal person. He was born in the Twenty-Fifth Plane, remember, where the ratio is faster than ours."

"And you actually believe he will be clever enough to overcome this mathematical fault which may engulf us all?"

"Yes. I cannot forget that look on his face when he transported us back to the normal world. He did it, Vi. I'll swear to it, and I regard that as just a glimpse of what he will be when mature. Why not, when you consider his ancestry? Yourself, Quorne, Viona, and me? I think Quorne is sure too that Sefian will solve the mystery, which is one reason why he's not concerning himself."

"If that is the case, it is pointless for us to hammer our heads on a brick wall. We had better find a way of tracing where Quorne finally settles and from then on keep in touch."

"You have an aura-compass reading of him, haven't you?"

"I did have, but since his transference by Brodix—and now back again—the compass no longer responds. Quorne's makeup has been altered considerably."

They went into the house and had the robot bring

a meal for them and they spoke but little as they ate. Then as a slight sound came from the direction of the French window, the Amazon glanced up in surprise. It could hardly be an intruder, since the house was ringed with invisible beams connected to alarms.

A second later the French window flew open from a violent impact and on the threshold stood the most incredible creature the Amazon or Abna had ever seen. They were so astounded they could only stare fixedly.

The visitor was no more than two feet tall and literally as broad as long—more like a cube than a living being, and supported on two immensely thick stumps with a gristly appendage corresponding to a human foot. The head and arms were merely extensions of the cube, and jointed so that they could shoot out telescopically to twice their normal length. The face of the creature was magnetically impressive. Completely square, with a vicious mouth, two small air intakes acting as a nose, and enormous eyes oddly like those of a cat. They had no lashes, which served to increase their hypnotic intensity.

The Amazon and Abna moved forward, only to stop as the unknown levelled a curious-looking weapon shaped like a trident.

"Do not move!" he commanded

His enunciation was perfect and spoken in a rumbling bass. There was a faint glimpse of pointed teeth as the lips writhed back in speaking

"Who are you?" Abna demanded.

"Avia of Zanji," the creature retorted. "I am one of

the many. On Earth now there are—" He hesitated at a mathematical point, then finished: "There are millions of us. We are the invincible ones."

Abna exchanged a quick glance with the Amazon. Both of them were thinking the same thing—that in all their travels throughout the System, and to worlds beyond it, they had never encountered a creature like this. Apparently, too, he was not without conceit.

"Invincible, eh?" Abna said, striding forward. "We shall see—"

He lashed out his hand and seized the claw-like hand holding the weapon. His intention was to hurl the small interloper from his feet—which normally, with his huge strength, be would have done quite easily. Instead, however, the free hand of the creature shot out on his extension forearm, clutched Abna's own wrist, and crushed with titanic power. Abna gasped and pain masked his features as he felt the bone grind to powder.

Abruptly released, he stumbled away, fighting mentally against the anguish of his shattered hand and wrist. Then, gradually, with his superb mastery over the vagaries of matter, he righted the condition and his shattered bones began to knit back into shape

The unknown watched the performance with an unblinking stare, as a cat might contemplate a cornered mouse. The Amazon, who had been on the verge of throwing her own superhuman strength into an attack, now hesitated.

"Fools," the creature said coldly. "How can you hope by physical means to struggle with such as me? Zanji is a world where one of your ounces would weigh a ton. We, born upon it, are possessed of strength beyond your imagination. As witness!"

With that Avia clenched his free hand and brought it down with a terrific impact upon the tungsten-alloy table at which Abna and the girl had been dining. The crockery and silverware flew in all directions and the hard metal top was dented and then at a second blow revealed a complete hole. With two smashing impacts of his fist this incredible creature had broken through metal which normally needed an acetylene flame when cutting was required.

"Where," the Amazon asked, "is Zanji? Who are you? What do you want here?"

"I have already told you I am one of millions. We are all over this world at the moment, dominating it, destroying those who oppose us. We have decided to pause here for a while in our journey from the Dark Tide. Zanji, our world, was on the point of being overwhelmed by the Dark when we left it. Now we are here, the first populated planet we have reached which is suitable for our type of life."

Avia had spoken the truth. He was one of a vast army of the creatures who had arrived in a colossal fleet of space machines, machines built of a polarizing metal and therefore virtually invisible.

At the moment Avia was speaking the powerful hordes were invading every city, wiping out opposition wherever they came upon it, taking control by virtue of the surprise of their arrival and their complete ruthlessness. How many space machines had arrived after a journey across space infinitely faster than light can travel, nobody knew. And nowhere had an alarm sounded. The beings of Zanji were scientists and capable of dealing with all scientific means of detection.

Sefner Quorne and Viona were also visited. When it happened, they were in the laboratory attached to the house. It had not taken Quorne long to take over the home he had once used during his earlier experiences on Earth. Legally it was still his, and therefore untenanted.

Now he and Viona stood staring as a man of Zanji came in upon them. The laboratory's outer door, for all its metal fastenings, was hanging on one hinge, smashed out of shape by two blows of the creature's fist.

"Come with me," the creature said, when he had explained himself. "I must take you to my superiors."

"Where are they?" Quorne asked sharply.

"In the nearest city. By now they will have taken control of it. Come!"

Viona began to move quietly in the direction of the inner door, her thoughts upon her son sleeping peacefully upstairs.

"You speak our language perfectly," Quorne commented. "I assume you read thoughts and transpose them into your own type of speech?"

"We are not telepathic," the creature retorted. "We learned your language over radio waves on our journey to—"

Suddenly the creature broke off. He had noticed that Viona was nearly at the door. Instantly he sprang forward, his vast weight making the stone floor quiver.

Reaching Viona, he caught savagely at her arm—then with a howl of pain he released her just as suddenly and crashed with stunning force to the floor. Chippings of stone flew in all directions from beneath his body.

Viona stared blankly, and so did Quorne. Then they looked at each other.

"What did you do?" Quorne asked, striding over to her.

"Why—nothing. He caught hold of me and—I just don't understand it."

Quorne hesitated, then he seized the body and tried to move it. Finally he had to give up, perspiration dewing his face.

"What are you trying to do, Sefner?" Viona asked.

"Do? I want to turn this body over and see if there's a heart or something. It shouldn't be in his back with an anatomy like this. If you killed him, I want to find out why."

Viona moved forward, stooped, and then braced herself. Slender though the appeared, she succeeded by a sudden effort in turning the creature on to his back. Then she stood up, breathing hard.

"Definitely you are a true daughter of your mother," Quorne said grudgingly; then going down on his knees, he examined the body carefully with instruments. When his examination was complete, he sat back on his heels and considered.

"Is he dead?" Viona asked.

"Yes. Either he had a sudden failure of the heart, or there was something about you that wiped him out. I must investigate further."

"Wouldn't it be safer to get away from here? If more of them come...."

"I am hoping, my dear, you may be able to deal with them," Quorne said.

He went to work with various scientific instruments, using some of them on the corpse and some of them on the girl. By the time his investigation was complete, half an hour had passed and he was smiling dourly to himself.

"My dear, you know what a catalyst is?" he asked, setting aside the detectors.

"Of course! A catalyst is a substance that reacts strangely on another substance. It produces certain effects without being changed itself."

"Exactly. Usually a catalyst is referred to in the case of metals. In this case it can be related to flesh and blood.... You, Viona, are a catalyst. And a fatal one, as far as this specimen from Zanji is concerned."

"But I don't understand!" Viona protested.

"As a scientist you should!" Quorne snapped. "There is an electrical content in your body, just as there is in any living creature, but it is of such an order as to be fatally powerful to the stressed molecules making up this man of Zanji. Presumably, all his colleagues are of the same basic constitution, so you will be fatal to all of them. The explanation is not hard to understand. You are not a natural human being."

Viona gave Quorne a half-angry glance.

"I mean," Quorne elaborated, "that you were not born in the normal way. You were produced by a fusion of mental forces emanated by the Amazon and Abna, your parents. Your electrical makeup is totally different from that of a naturally-born human. You do not affect other people strangely, but you certainly are as dangerous as a high tension wire to creatures like this!"

Viona wrinkled her forehead. She could grasp the scientific implication easily enough, but its possibilities troubled her.

"I foresee tremendous power in my hands," Quorne mused, "with you as my bargaining weapon."

"You seem to have forgotten that I am also your wife!"

"Of course you are, my dear—and what a wife! Due to your hitherto unsuspected gift, you can give me what I have always sought—mastery of the system! Get the child, Viona. We are going to London, since that is obviously where these creatures have taken control. I think I can make a bargain with the invaders."

"By using me? No, Sefner, I won't do it!"

Quorne turned slowly, his eyes pinning Viona relentlessly.

"Viona, do not ever make the mistake of telling me what you will do. I arrange your movements, your life. I married you because I believed I could thereby have a child to continue my rulership when I have built it up. You belong to me, and will always do as I command. Now get the child!"

Viona hesitated. At moments like these she was brought to the bitter realization that her mother, the Amazon, had been only too right. Quorne had not a spark of love, or even sentiment in his makeup.

"Go!" Quorne ordered angrily

Completely dominated, Viona had to obey. She went upstairs, dressed herself for the outdoors, then wrapped up the sleeping child and brought it down with her. She found Quorne outside, waiting in the car.

"We may have an uninterrupted journey to London," he said. "I do not see any more of the invaders about. Get in."

Viona did so, a blank look in her blue eyes. Quorne gave a final glance over the darkened, secured house and then settled at the wheel.

CHAPTER SIX
HURLED INTO SPACE

Meantime, Abna and the Amazon had recovered a little from their first shock and were waiting to see what Avia would do next.

"Come with me," he said. "My superiors will question you."

"Apparently we have no choice," the Amazon said. "But first I must switch off various apparatus in my laboratory. I might ruin valuable experiments otherwise—experiments that might also interest your superiors."

The baleful eyes of the man from Zanji became suspicious for a moment, and then he relaxed.

"I will go with you to the laboratory," he said. "Proceed."

The Amazon flashed a brief, meaning glance at Abna. He understood and moved over to her, staying at her side as she left the room with the invader close behind them, gun in hand, the floor quaking under his ponderous footfalls.

In the laboratory the Amazon moved to an instrument on a solidly built tripod. The Zanjian looked at it curiously, moving closer to do so as the Amazon turned the switches—then suddenly he cried out as he found himself rooted to the floor, his weapon dropping out of his hand. Though his weird eyes glared blue murder, there was nothing he could do. He was as solidly fixed as though in a casing of stone.

"Evidently our conceited friend is not so smart as he thinks," the Amazon said, glancing at Abna. "We have nothing to fear from him as long as this instrument remains on. He is completely paralyzed."

Abna nodded absently, studying the little, immensely heavy being as he walked around him. Avia remained motionless, his iron strength held in thrall by the paralyzing electromagnetic waves generated by the Amazon's projector.

"That the menace of the Dark is a real, deadly thing we now know without doubt," the Amazon commented. "Otherwise this creature and his race would never have forsaken their own world on the rim of the Dark and flown here for brief sanctuary. Apparently the world of Zanji is one we've never encountered."

"It must be exceptionally dense material," Abna said. "This creature said an ounce on his world would weigh a ton. Quite possible, of course. Eddington, to mention only one of the Earth scientists, stated long ago that heat is not entirely necessary for compressibility of matter. Continued pressure on this being's world, caused perhaps by internal atomic disintegration, would finally produce a mass of matter with its shell of satellite electrons stripped. In other words, the same amount of matter in an exceptionally small space. Beings on such a world would conform to the gravity, producing a creature like this."

"He must be capable of being killed," the Amazon said. "And should be—together with as many more of his fellows as we can find. This might be a good chance to find what is fatal to his type of constitution. Paralysis is not enough in itself."

With her usual ruthlessness when confronted by an enemy, the Amazon turned to the laboratory's various instruments and considered them. Finally she selected an electric gun, which jetted forth a stream of disintegrative energy when she pressed the button. But to her amazement, it had no effect on the man from Zanji. He remained motionless, his muscles paralyzed, but there was not a mark on his skin to show where the energy had struck him.

"I think you're wasting your time, Vi," Abna said. "Matter only disintegrates when it is normal matter. Here we have it in its densest, most compressed state—the hard core of matter itself. I doubt if there is an energy in existence which will shatter it."

The Amazon's yellow face hardened and she turned again to her instruments. She tried various things—heat, acids, even a small type of atomic shell, but the armour-plate skin of the invader remained unhurt.

"Now I know why he called himself invincible," she said at length. "He is so tough he can't be killed—not by our type of destructive weapons, anyway. Yet he must have an Achilles' heel. His muscles can be locked—as you see—so he must be capable of being destroyed."

"I can try breaking him down by mental force," Abna suggested, but the Amazon shook her head.

"That is not what we want, Abna. Presumably these beings have wrested control of this planet and we have to find a way to unseat and destroy them. Even if you could break down this creature, you couldn't possibly deal with armies of them. We need something concrete."

"Then there is only one solution. Analyze him and find out his exact makeup. When we have that we can, mathematically, find something which will break him down."

The Amazon nodded promptly and proceeded to set a battery of analytical machines around the immovable creature. Then she and Abna went to work noting down every reaction—until by the time they had finished they knew the creature's exact energy content, his temperature, his nervous system, his heartbeats and respiration—every biological detail.

But to know these things was no help whatever for, according to the computer, the type of energy needed to destroy his life could not be created in a laboratory.

"Just as he said, invincible," Abna said grimly, when he and the Amazon had been forced to the truth. "The type of energy we need to destroy him and his fellows is unknown to us. It might exist somewhere in the void as a free agent, but that is obviously a hopeless proposition. It begins to look as though this creature and his fellows have absolute power to do as they like, and we can do nothing to stop them."

"Do you suppose they could withstand super-x bombs hurled in their midst?" the Amazon asked, and Abna gave a start.

"You mean bomb them out?"

"If it is the only method, yes. Even their form of matter will surely not be able to stand atomic bombs in triple-ratio?"

"Perhaps not, but what of the ordinary people? They will be wiped out, too. Cities will topple. All the civilization of this planet will be reduced to ruin—and even then we shall not be rid of all these creatures."

"True, but if we can smash down some of them, we may break the spell about their being invincible and that might lead them to hurrying on into the void again to escape the Dark. We must do something, Abna, and that is all I can suggest at the moment."

"When do we do it?" Abna questioned.

"Tonight—now, before the creatures get too strong a grip. I have a small air-space machine in the hangar outside. It won't take ten minutes to load it with super-x bombs."

Since the Amazon had plainly made up her mind, Abna said no more. He helped her to load up the machine with the small but unthinkably powerful explosives then—leaving Avia still under the influence of the paralyzer—they entered the super-fast flyer and settled at the control board. Within a few minutes its atomic jets had hurtled it at stupendous velocity into the night sky.

Down below there was nothing visible except the grey, indeterminate surface of the Earth lighted by a high full moon. Abna switched on the night screens that gave daylight renderings of everything below. Fields and villages came into view—then here and there appeared a long, cigar-like object with portholes. They appeared to be scattered pretty freely all the way to the blaze of lights that marked London.

"How many hordes there are we don't know," the Amazon said at last, "but what they have to learn is that this world is not entirely without science. A few super-x bombs smashed into the middle of London, where they will undoubtedly be congregated in fairly considerable numbers, should wake them up a bit."

"And the ordinary men and women who have been overwhelmed by this sudden attack? You mean to destroy them, too?"

"I cannot single them out, can I?" The Amazon gave a shrug. "The human race increases quickly, Abna— all too quickly. A little thinning out will do no harm."

"And if Viona should be down there in the city? We don't know where Quorne took her, remember."

The Amazon hesitated, then she seemed to steel herself.

"If she is down there, she must suffer with the rest. She has chosen her own course: I cannot discriminate. Quorne will be with her."

Abna caught at the Amazon's shoulder. "Look, Vi. Do you realize what you are saying? You—"

He broke off, suddenly catching sight of curling "S" lines of sparks sweeping up from the lighted haze of the mighty metropolis below.

"Rocket ships," he said quickly, "probably coming for us."

The Amazon nodded tautly. "We'll give them a taste of what we can do before they reach us. Get to the guns."

Abna hurried to the protonic cannon, checking its mechanism quickly and then shifting the prismatic sights so the upsweeping machines, detectable only by their fiery exhausts, could be brought into range. At the same moment the Amazon pressed her yellow finger on the bomb release button and the indicator revealed one of the terrible explosives had left its rack.

For a moment the Amazon was reminded of a time many years before when she had attacked London to achieve domination: it struck her as odd that now she was attacking it to prevent another power doing exactly the same thing. But she felt happy again—happy in the knowledge that she would have to fight and use her scientific genius against a race obviously devoid of all sentiment.

The bomb struck home in the center of the pool of myriad lights. Even at this great height the airwaves tremored under the concussion and, below, the night was more brilliant for an instant than a dozen noon-days.

"Smack in the middle!" Abna exclaimed, turning for a moment. "Nice work—"

He would probably have said more, but at that instant the attackers came zooming up out of the gulf. Evidently, they were using their own particular form of scientific attack, for instead of beaming forth with energy rays or heat-beams, both of which they could have counteracted, they used a brilliantly vivid pencil of blue white flame, its glare infinitely more intense than that of an acetylene core.

The Amazon closed her eyes against the fierce brilliance and groped around for blue goggles on the rack beside her. She slipped them in place and reopened her eyes. The pencil, to her vision, had now dimmed sufficiently to be looked upon. Others abruptly joined it, all fixing immovably to the flyer despite the Amazon's frantic efforts with the controls to pull free.

Abna, half-blinded, shouted: "Give me a chance to get below them out of range of those beams."

"I'm doing all I can. I think," the Amazon added, "that those beams have magnetic qualities and are anchored to our vessel no matter where I swing it. Listen!"

Abna looked up sharply, blinking, at the sound of twanging metal and the dull clink of plates fissuring.

"The machine's giving way!" he cried.

A gaping hole appeared in the side of the flyer. Immediately the air whistled out of the control cabin, and the colder, more rarefied air began to enter. Abna left his weapon and stumbled to the Amazon as she sat at the controls.

He said urgently: "We can't shake free of these

beams and so far I haven't got in one retaliatory burst."

"If only I had my *Ultra* instead of this crate," the Amazon muttered. "I'd give these invaders something—"

"But we haven't got the *Ultra*, Vi, and this ship's falling to bits all around us. We've got to bale out!"

He brought parachutes and harnesses, handed one over and began to buckle on the other.

"They might as well have a final reminder," the Amazon said, and she snapped all the switches of the bomb-rack one after the other.

Seconds passed, then the upheaval of five Super-x bombs crashing into the city below had their reaction above. The flyer tossed and bounced like a rubber ball in a stormy sea, and yet the beams, obviously magnetic, remained chained to it, eating through the metal as if with powerful acids.

"I suppose we're leaping into captivity," the Amazon said, pulling open the slide door. "But there's nothing else for it. At least we'll sell ourselves dearly."

She took one of the proton guns from the wall rack, then with it in her hand she jumped out into space, pulling the ripcord with her free hand after the required interval.

Her headlong flight was checked and she began to drift, lower and lower, down toward the vast fires raging where the bombs had dropped.

CHAPTER SEVEN
QUORNE HOLDS THE REINS

She found herself dropping to the rear of a blast-shattered building some distance away from the heart of the atomic fires now raging where the bombs had fallen. She flexed her knees and dropped without hurt, quickly casting off her harness

She looked around and above her. A dim white shape faintly visible was drifting downwards. It fell with the wind drift a dozen yards away, and the Amazon hurried across as Abna disentangled himself.

"Take a look," he said, nodding. "Our friends up there have still got our machine nailed—or what's now left of it."

The Amazon only glanced at the pencils in the sky: she had other things on her mind.

"Best thing we can do is try to strike toward the space port, providing my bombing didn't destroy it, and see if we can locate the *Ultra*. Once within that we can probably hold out indefinitely."

Abna nodded and they began moving side by side, watching the flickering glare not far away and catching the sounds of vehicles, sirens, and the higher note of humanity on the move. Just how many invaders there were in London, and how firmly their control was rooted, neither the Amazon nor Abna had any idea as yet.

Then two invaders loomed ahead. The Amazon had fired before she realized that normal weapons were useless on these heavy-matter beings—then she found herself seized and hurled to the ground. At the same moment Abna also went down. Concerned only with herself, the Amazon lashed out with all her strength, driving her fist repeatedly into the face of the squat being pinning her down. She dealt blows that would have smashed the jaw of any ordinary man, but upon this creature she had little effect. So she tried to squirm free, using her immense strength to try to break the grip on her shoulders that was pinning her down. But she struggled to no avail, and at last had to give up, panting and furious. Only then did the man from Zanji permit her to get up, his gun ready. Abna, whose gigantic strength had availed him nothing, was also allowed to rise.

"You are both strong," one of the men said. "Stronger than any we have yet encountered—but you cannot defeat the invincible ones. Come with us to head-quarters."

The Amazon said nothing, permitting herself to be seized by the arm and led amidst the rubble of shattered buildings, Abna close in the rear in charge of the other guard—until at length the approximate center of the city was reached. Here there was chaos supreme. Buildings were leaning drunkenly, some of them blasted to mere shells. Monstrous chasms gaped in the roadways. Men and women were milling around aimlessly, some of them watched by the men of Zanji—distinguishable in the flickering glow by their squat forms—and others moving about freely, evidently realizing they could not escape even if they tried.

The guards holding Abna and the Amazon seemed nonplussed at first at the chaos around them, then as they got on the move again they came to less devastated regions where huge buildings still stood unscathed. One of them the Amazon recognized as the government headquarters, and into it she and Abna were taken, being marched through lines of guards standing with weapons in hand along the entrance hall.

They went finally into one of the large lower rooms. Here were more Zanjian guards against the walls, and in the center of the room at a big desk—the Prime Minister's—sat two figures. One was obviously a man of Zanji, with attire more elaborate than any they'd seen so far, and the other an Earth man.... No, not an Earth man as such, but resembling one.

"Quorne!" the Amazon exclaimed, coming to a halt in amazement.

"I can imagine your surprise," Quorne said drily, and a motion of his hand left the Amazon and Abna free to move forward.

"So this invasion is your idea?" Abna demanded, reaching the desk. "Just the kind of thing you would manage to contrive, Quorne!"

Quorne shook his head. "You do me an injustice, Abna. I had nothing to do with it—and if you care to read my mind you will realize I am speaking the truth. Usually I keep my mind a blank against your probings, but this time—"

"I think he's speaking the truth, Abna," the Amazon interrupted. "These invaders wouldn't be here at all but for that dark tide advancing from space. I'm satisfied of that. The mystery is how you, Quorne, came to be seated next to this creature. I assume he is a dignitary of his race?"

"The ruler," the creature himself corrected. "I and the Earthman are jointly controlling this planet."

The Amazon's attention switched back to Quorne.

"You couldn't have achieved this position by ordinary methods, Quorne. Just how have you managed to get yourself a joint supreme authority?"

"I owe it to your daughter, Amazon—and yours, Abna. A most useful girl! She has given me the one thing I want, control of the system."

"She has!" Abna echoed. "You're lying, Quorne! Viona may have gone the wrong way when she was forced to marry you, but I'm certain she'd never agree to your plans for conquest of the system, let alone help you."

Quorne sat back in his chair, his sardonic face amused.

"She is in the position that she cannot help herself."

The Amazon looked puzzled, then the ruler of Zanji started speaking, and the more he talked the more annoyed Quorne looked.

"The woman Sefner Quorne speaks of is a power to be reckoned with," the ruler said. "One touch of her finger, no more—and we of Zanji die. Possessing such power as that, I have no alternative but to agree to the terms of this Earth man."

"He is not an Earth man born," Abna retorted. "Jupiter is his native planet, as it is mine. This man was once my adviser when my kingdom flourished. He turned traitor. Now he is a seeker of power and to obtain it he will destroy everything on his path, including you."

The eyes of the creature slanted towards Quorne, but by this time the scientist had become impassive again. Then the Amazon took up the conversation, addressing herself to Quorne.

"What does he mean about Viona? How can she possibly make these ironhard men die by merely touching them?"

"You are a scientist, Amazon," Quorne retorted. "Why not try to discover for yourself?"

"We don't need to," Abna said, who had been studying Quorne intently in the interval. "You've been leaving your mind unmasked and from your thoughts I can see that Viona is an electrical catalyst."

"She's—what?" The Amazon cried.

"According to Quorne's thoughts, Viona has natu-rally the very thing we need—an electrical energy capable of upsetting the constitution of these Zanjians."

"Correct," Quorne agreed, realizing there was no

further point in concealing the truth. "I discovered it by accident and brought Viona to this city. I have made a bargain with Kron, whom you see at my side.... In return for their immunity from Viona's peculiar power—for she has only to walk amongst the Zanjians and touch them to wipe them out—I have obtained mastery of the Earth along with Kron. We will exchange notes and act as we deem fit. He will also help me in the conquest of the entire System."

"I cannot understand why Viona is not killed and the threat to the Zanjians wiped out," the Amazon said, frowning.

"There are many reasons," Quorne replied. "For one thing the Zanjians are not averse to my joining them. It is always useful to have a member of an invaded race at your side who can tell you many things you do not yourself know. Then there is the matter of Sefian. The child is with Viona, and will remain with her. The Zanjians know as we do that if the child is to be kept alive, and his immense knowledge to be of benefit in the future, then his mother must also keep alive. If she dies, so does Sefian."

"Why?" the Amazon asked, astonished. That Quorne was talking nonsense was perfectly obvious. The death of Viona could not automatically bring about Sefian's death—but the Amazon did not pursue the subject. Quorne had obviously talked the uninitiated ruler of the Zanjians into believing his story, and since it meant that Viona would remain unharmed because of it the Amazon had no intention of enlightening Kron.

"Where is Viona now?" Abna asked.

"Safe enough, where I can call on her whenever I need."

"And the dark menace from space? Have you thought any more about that? You have proof enough now of its reality since these Zanjians are trying to escape from it."

"Sefian will solve that problem," Quorne said calmly. "For my own part I am turning my attention, with the aid of these men of Zanji, to the mastery of the System. We have many plans to lay, of course. The peoples of this planet, incidentally, have been taken by surprise. Power has been stripped from every Earthman and woman who possessed it and Zanjians have replaced them.... I can see my dream coming true," Quorne continued, musing. "I have a race of scientists here, completely unsentimental, who will be at one with me in the plan I have for conquest. Before I always lacked sufficient numbers of an intelligent species to work with me. Now the path is wide open in front of me."

"Take care there isn't an abyss at the end of it," the Amazon warned. "Do you think for a moment these scientists will tolerate you once you have told them all they want to know?"

"You forget, Amazon, I have Viona and Sefian as my insurance. I can achieve all I need while they remain."

Kron started speaking, his bleak, lashless eyes moving to the Amazon, and then Abna.

"Both of you are scientists," he said. "I have learned as much from Sefner Quorne—and both of you are very dangerous on that account. I assume you were responsible for the atomic explosions that occurred a while ago? You destroyed the heart of this city, and it will take a good deal of rebuilding. Were you not so dangerous with your knowledge, you would be set to work with the men and women who will do the rebuilding. Because of your scientific power, however, you must be annihilated."

The Amazon flashed a quick look at Quorne.

"Quorne, are you content to sit back and see this creature, or some members of his race, destroy us?" she demanded.

"Certainly. We are not exactly in love with each other, are we?"

"You have married my daughter. That ought to make for some kind of tie."

"None at all, Amazon. Your daughter is not a natural woman. I have nothing for you except bitter enmity and the most profound respect. I might say the same to you, Abna."

"Quorne," the Amazon said deliberately, "you're a short-sighted fool! Possibly these creatures will allow Sefian to mature and refrain from destroying Viona because of what you have told them—but do you believe for one moment they will tolerate you when the mastery of the system has been achieved, you handing them knowledge when they ask for it? They'll blot you out."

"Stop wasting your time, Amazon," Quorne said. "I know exactly what I am doing, and the sooner you and

Abna are removed from my path, the better I'll like it."

The Amazon gave a desperate glance about her as Kron signalled to two of the guards by the wall.

"So many times you have escaped when I have planned your demise, Amazon, that I think it would be better this time for me to watch it take place," Quorne said. "I will at least permit it to be swift. One blast from the raygun and—" He spread his hands and smiled cynically.

CHAPTER EIGHT
OFF TO URANIAN WILDS

Kron nodded to the guards, and immediately they whipped their weapons from their pockets and aimed them.

But at that moment Viona entered the room. She paused, her blue eyes looking coldly at Quorne—then she moved them to the Amazon and Abna. The guards lowered their weapons, uncertain what to do.

"What do you want?" Quorne shouted, springing to his feet. "I thought I told you to stay away from me!"

"From the appearance of things in here, it's as well I did not," Viona retorted.

She came forward and spoke to the guards.

"Get back to your places!" she commanded, and it was sufficient for her to move toward them to send them hurrying away on two-ton feet.

"You've no right here!" Quorne insisted, his livid face betraying how deep was his rage. "What of Sefian? How dare you leave him with these Zanjians everywhere?"

"He won't be hurt—and you know it. The Zanjians place too much store on his future possibilities. Nor will I be hurt either, because if I die—so does he."

Quorne looked as though he could not understand the girl's attitude—as, indeed, he could not. It was the first time she had ever taken him to task. It made it doubly worse when the Amazon and Abna were looking on, grimly smiling. Kron, for his part, had not the power to betray himself by expressions, so he just stared with his hideous lashless eyes.

Quorne said, his voice measured: "You had better leave! Now!"

His heliotrope eyes bored into the girl's as he spoke, full of the intensity of hypnotic power—but, though Viona caught at the edge of the desk to steady herself, she did not break down. From somewhere she found the strength of will to resist.

"I have ceased doing as you ask, Sefner," she answered. "I shall never again do as you ask. It has taken me a long time to find out what kind of a man you are—and now I have done so, I'm horrified. I was going to say all this in private, but I don't see why you should be spared like that, particularly as my mother and father happen to be here. And Kron may like to know, too."

Quorne came round the desk, catching Viona's shoulders fiercely.

"Viona, you little fool, do you realize what you're doing? Saying? If you have some difference to settle, then let us do it alone."

"I'm doing it here!" Viona insisted, her voice rising. "I want everybody, Kron included, to know what kind of a man you are! You've used me as a weapon against these invaders, and now you'll use my son to further your own mad dream of conquering the System. Just as you'll use Kron and his race. You'll learn all you can from them and then, probably helped by Sefian's knowledge when he grows up, you'll wipe out the Zanjian race and—"

Quorne, his fury spilling over; struck her savagely across the face. She reeled away, stumbled, and nearly overbalanced.

"Maybe that will teach you to behave yourself!" Quorne shouted. "How dare you come in here and—"

Quorne stopped, realizing the view of Viona, her cheek flaming, had been blocked by the Amazon. He dropped his hand to his gun, but in one catlike bound the Amazon was upon him, her hands at his throat. He was whirled around helplessly and then flung with devastating force backwards. He made a frantic grab at the desk to save himself, missed, and finally sat down on the floor.

Regardless of guns, Kron, and everything else, the Amazon darted after him, whirled him up effortlessly with one yellow hand, then used the other to slap him back and forth across the face with fiendish impacts. Behind each blow was the full force of the Amazon's superhuman strength, and Quorne felt as if his universe were exploding in stars and ribbons of light.

"Stop!" Kron's voice ordered. *"Stop!"*

The Amazon heard. She ceased the slapping and instead lashed up a left hook. It crashed straight into

Quorne's chin, lifted him off his feet, then dropped him helplessly on his face. He lay groaning, his jaw broken, blood trickling from his nostrils after the battering he had received.

"You, Amazon, will pay for this," Kron said, coming round the desk with his gun ready. "You cannot treat the co-ruler of the world in this fashion."

"I have already done so," the Amazon retorted. "And next time I'll kill him."

"There will be no next time," Kron assured her, and then raised his hand to signal his guards. But before he could do so, Viona hurried forward, putting herself between her mother and father and holding on to their arms.

"Kill my parents and I will kill myself!" she said, her eyes defiant. "You know what that will mean— the death of my son, on whom you're pinning so many hopes."

Kron motioned his hand slightly and the guards retreated.

"I am in the difficult position, Viona Quorne, that I do not know whether your husband has spoken the truth or not," he said. "Biologically, I cannot see why the death of a parent should entail the death of an offspring, but there remains the possibility that it might apply to your particular species. In any event, I cannot take the chance."

Viona relaxed a little, then cast a glance at Quorne as he began to make movements to pick himself up from the floor.

"When my husband has recovered, he can tell you where I am should I be needed," Viona said. "Until then, I am taking my parents with me."

Kron hesitated, but there was nothing he could do with Viona's threat still holding him at bay. She moved to the door with the Amazon and Abna on either side of her. Out in the corridor the guards looked on, but knowing Viona was deadly to them, they made no attempt to interfere. In any case they had no orders to do so.

"Come with me," Viona murmured quickly, as the Amazon and Abna glanced at her inquiringly. "We should be able to get away."

She led them to the end of the corridor and so to the street.

"Those bombs of yours threw the Zanjian's plans into complete disorder, mother," Viona said. "I doubt if they'll ever get their grip back. People know now what they're up against and they may have time to organise resistance. However, our own safety is the most important thing at the moment. We'll be safe in my car."

Viona nodded to a powerful atom car. "Kron permitted me to have it after Sefner had made his bargain. It enables me to move about with speed and safety. That insignia on the front makes it official."

As they hurried down the steps towards it, the Amazon and Abna both noted the curiously fashioned pennant on the nose of the car, then they had climbed in, Viona taking the wheel. It was difficult to make progress, but at length she reached one of the out-town roads and drove fast.

"Just where are we going?" the Amazon asked. "Your hideout?"

"Yes—if you can call it that. It's home really—the house Sefner has always had. Kron guaranteed it immunity."

"I wonder," Abna said slowly, "how long that immunity will last? When Quorne has recovered, he'll not have any reason to love you any more, Viona. He'll probably tell Kron the truth—that your death would not prevent Sefian going on living."

"I fully expect it," the girl answered. "That is why I intend to get out as quickly as possible, and take Sefian with me. I've made the break with Sefner, with the bitter realization that you were right from the very start."

Abna and the Amazon exchanged grim glances in the glow of the roof light, and after that Viona spoke but little. Finally the dark residence that belonged to Quorne was reached. They went in and Viona switched on lights.

"I am staying only long enough to get Sefian," she said. "It would be presumptuous of me to ask if you can fend for yourselves against whatever might happen next, so—"

"Where," the Amazon interrupted, "do you intend going? Since it seems these Zanjians have settled all over the world and are exerting their domination, you won't get very far if Quorne decides that you ought to be wiped out."

"He'll have to follow me to Uranus if he wants me," Viona replied.

"Uranus?" Abna gave a start. "So you're flying into space? But why Uranus? Nobody knows anything about that world as yet."

"That's why I'm going there. You know I'm never happy unless I'm exploring." Viona laid a gentle hand on her parents' arms. "I want to say I'm sorry," she continued. "Sorry for acting like a fool when you tried to point out what kind of a man I'd married. I've grown up a good deal since then and I've seen for myself.... I can only say one thing in my own defence: Sefner made me marry him: I had no choice."

"Do you mean," the Amazon asked, "that you intend to bring up young Sefian amidst the wilds of Uranus? The dark tide advancing from space will be on us in a few more years, and Uranus will be blotted out before Earth. Wouldn't you do better to stay with your father and me?"

"Doing what?"

"Helping us to wipe out these Zanjians," the Amazon snapped. "And your husband, too. So far I have held my hand in regard to him because of you: now I am no longer tied. He and the Zanjians together form one of the biggest menaces Earth has ever faced."

"How do we destroy it?" Abna asked, his face grim. "We know already that all ordinary methods fail."

"Yes, but we know that Viona has the key. To the Zanjians she is poison."

Viona gave a troubled smile. "I'm well aware of

that fact. Sefner used it as his bargaining weapon—but I am certainly not going to stay on Earth and turn myself into a destroyer of these invaders. In any case, I wouldn't be. I'd lose my life. And it would make me feel like a murderess."

"I am afraid, my dear, you are too sentimentally human in some things," the Amazon sighed. "Maybe, as you grow older, you will realize that sentiment has no part in the world today. There is only the age-old law—destroy, or be destroyed. However, I would not wish you to expose yourself to the deadly danger of being a destroyer. There's another way, granting we have the time to arrange it."

"Another way?"

"I suppose this house has a laboratory?" the Amazon asked.

Viona nodded and led the way by a connecting doorway, down a passage, and then into the laboratory where she and Quorne had made their first encounter with a man of Zanji. He still lay on the stone floor where he had fallen.

"What idea have you in mind?" Abna inquired, as the Amazon quickly considered the various instruments.

"Just this. Any particular form of energy in the universe can be duplicated, but you must of course know its formula first. We are fortunate in learning that Viona's own bodily energy is exactly of the right wavelength to destroy the makeup of these invaders. We must analyze Viona, discover what the energy wavelength is, and then duplicate it with electrical apparatus. Once we have done that, we have a weapon—one which can get these Zanjians on the run."

Abna nodded. "Excellent idea—and the sooner the better. You have no objections, Viona?"

"None," the girl assented promptly. "Providing we can get the analysis made before anybody catches up with us."

The Amazon turned quickly to the instruments, understanding some but not others, until presently she came upon an electrical analyzer,

"This is it!" she exclaimed, switching on its self-powered generators. "Here, Viona, take these in your hands."

Viona obeyed, clenching her fingers around two thin rods resembling electrodes. Beyond a faint tingling as the circuit through her body was completed, she felt no discomfort. In silent wonder she watched the many dial faces with their needles swinging. One had a curious pointer that jerked up and down in tune with her heartbeats.

"We have it!" the Amazon said at last, her notes of the dial readings completed. "Thanks, Viona, that's all."

The girl handed back the electrodes and was about to hurry from the laboratory when Abna's voice checked her.

"A moment, Viona! In what do you intend to fly to Uranus? Have you a spaceship close at hand or do you have to risk finding one?"

"There's a small machine in the hangar adjoining this lab. Sefner kept it there in the event of sudden emergency. It will be big enough for Sefian and me, and it has plenty of fuel."

Viona turned and left. When the door had closed, the Amazon gave Abna a look as she raised her head from her notes.

"We could stop her," she said, "but I don't think it advisable. Uranus is a danger, of course—and so is space itself for that matter; but the danger on Earth here is even greater. For the sake of Viona, and as much for Sefian, maybe she had better carry out her plan. Meantime, we have a good deal to do building a projector to transmit this particular form of energy."

Abna turned to the bench, ready to commence work. For a while he was silent, fashioning the first stages of the transformer, while the Amazon set up the coil-windings.

"Do you suppose Viona will be allowed to go into space?" Abna asked. "Surely the guards will have orders to stop anybody trying to leave Earth?"

The Amazon thought for a moment, then she hurried from the laboratory. In the house she found that Viona was in flying kit, the sleeping Sefian in his blanket cradled in her right arm.

"In spite of this seeming like cowardice, I'm going," she said, glancing toward her mother.

"Cowardice?" the Amazon repeated. "No, my dear. It is not cowardice to protect the future—and that is what you are doing. Sefian is probably the only person who can save the System when the dark smudge becomes a real menace. Here," the Amazon added, handing over the pennant from the car, "display this at one of your observation windows. It gave your car immunity; maybe it will give it your space machine, too."

Viona took it with her free hand and smiled. "I was just wondering how to get around that problem. Thanks for solving it for me...." She hesitated and then kissed her mother gently, and afterwards Abna. "I'll keep in touch by radio," she said. "Waveband 892. Nobody else is likely to tune in to that."

"We'll see you off," the Amazon said, and opened the connecting door that led to the hangar.

CHAPTER NINE
AMAZON TO THE RESCUE

When Quorne finally found his battered senses returning to him, he slowly got on to his knees, then to his feet. Looking about him, he realized that the Zanjian guards were in their accustomed place by the wall and that Kron was at the desk, holding his oddly designed gun in his hand.

"You men of Earth are remarkably fragile," he commented as Quorne moved to the desk, dabbing at his cut face with a swab, and then holding his aching jaw.

"Any man would be fragile before the Golden Amazon!" Quorne said. "You have seen now for your-self what kind of a woman she is. Abna, her husband, is even stronger."

"Yet neither of them strong enough to break the invincible ones, Quorne."

"Possibly not. You are a particularly dense form of matter." Quorne sat down heavily and mopped his forehead, then looked about him. "Where is my wife? And the Amazon and Abna?"

"I was compelled to let them go. It was that, or let

your wife destroy herself."

"What!" Quorne leaped to his feet again. "Do you realize what you have done, Kron? The Amazon and Abna, as long as they are free, can endanger our whole scheme for the System! They are brilliant scientists and—"

"Had your wife carried out her threat and killed herself, or had I had her killed, your offspring Sefian, on whom we are relying so much, would have been lost to us. I could not take that risk."

"Nothing of the sort!" Quorne shouted, forgetting himself. "Sefian will go on living even if his mother does die! She deserves to die! She came here with a string of lies about me. She has outlived her usefulness and has too much of her mother, the Amazon, in her for my liking. She—"

Quorne stopped, then he went on again with a change in his voice. As usual, the relentless face of Kron had no expression, but there seemed to be a deadly look in the baleful eyes.

"Why do you point that gun at me? I'm unarmed. I can't do anything. Wouldn't it be more reasonable to find my wife and her parents and wipe out the lot of them?"

"They can be found easily enough whenever we want them. In the meantime, Quorne, I am wondering if your wife was not right."

"Right? About what?"

"She said you would use me and my race, learn everything possible from us, and then—helped by your son at maturity—you would wipe us all out."

"I know she said that, but it's ridiculous! She was on the verge of hysteria. You could see that for yourself."

"You stand condemned out of your own mouth as a liar, Quorne. You swore that the death of your wife would bring about the death of your son. Upon that our bargain partly rested. Because I was not certain whether or not you had spoken the truth, I had to let your wife and the two greatest potential dangers—the Golden Amazon and Abna—go free."

"You can find them again! You've just said so."

"I hope so. It would not even be necessary but for you. But for you, I would have had no need to make a bargain at all and share so many of my secret plans with you. I have no time for a liar. You might easily aim at the plan your wife outlined and later try to destroy us. I am resolved you shall learn no more—and do no more."

Quorne started to speak, then changed his mind. He saw his gun lying on the floor not far away and made a dive for it. Just as he reached it, Kron pressed the button of his weapon and then pressed it again. Quorne half rose from the floor and then he silently collapsed, arms sprawling. Kron contemplated him impassively for a moment and then went over to him. Without effort, he raised him up in one hand, studied him, and then threw him down again.

"Dispose of the body," he ordered curtly, motioning to the guards, and returned to his place at the desk.

From that moment he took no further interest

in the removal of the body. Once it had been taken from the room he pressed a button that plunged the place into darkness. The actuation of more switches and buttons brought a series of television screens into action and upon them were mirrored all the great cities of the world, some of them normally in darkness but made clear by infrared process. As he surveyed, Kron spoke through the microphone close at hand, giving his orders to those he had appointed his commanders immediately under him.

Only in London was there complete confusion, and the more he studied the ruins and the hurrying men and women—now and again pursued by men of his own race—the more his fury mounted. Finally he switched through to the Zanjian in charge of the London sector. After a moment the man's face appeared on the screen—expressionless, his eyes baleful.

"How much longer is it going to take you, Nilian, to bring order out of chaos?" Kron demanded. "We had everybody at our mercy and now I see them rushing about in all directions. In such disorder lies the seed of organized resistance."

"I am doing all I can, master," Nilian retorted. "But for the bombs dropped by the Golden Amazon this would never have happened."

"Don't find excuses: get the matter put right quickly!"

"It will not be easy, master. In the confusion, thousands of Earth people fled underground. We are doing our best to locate them."

"Use every available man," Kron ordered. "These

Earth people are not fools and they have a fair knowledge of science. If they organize themselves into a resistant army we shall face considerable difficulty, even more so if the Golden Amazon or Abna of Jupiter should help them. You must also use as many men as possible to find the Amazon and Abna. They departed with the wife of Sefner Quorne over an hour ago."

"We will endeavour to trace them, master."

Impatiently, Kron switched off and sat thinking for a moment, aware more than any of his fellows that trying to trace scientists as efficient as the Amazon and Abna would be no simple task. Then in the midst of his preoccupation the signal buzzer sounded. He switched on.

"Speak! Kron, the master, is listening." It was Nilian again, his face merging into view on the communicator screen.

"I require instructions, master," he said. "A small space machine with your own insignia of immunity displayed has just crossed the Heaviside Layer headed for outer space. The air and spacelane guards gave it free passage: but now they have reported the matter to me I am wondering if they did correctly—"

"Fool! Idiot!" Kron shouted. "I gave orders that no ship was to leave Earth for the void! No ship at all! Understand? Have it followed instantly. Destroy it if need be. It cannot be any of our own people, so it may be the Golden Amazon or Abna, or even the wife of Quorne. Report to me when it has been annihilated."

"That may be some time, master. It is moving at

high speed."

"We have machines which can exceed the speed of light if necessary, so don't use that as an argument for failure. Hurry!"

Sliding back the shutters by pressure on a wall button, Kron gazed up into the night sky, but could see no trace of the space machine Nilian had referred to. Which was hardly to be wondered at, for Viona was well clear of the Heaviside Layer and hurtling her little flyer into the depths of space. She gave it the maximum speed she could endure, Sefian being stretched out flat on the wall bed, even his small body sinking considerably into the springs under the acceleration pressure.

For the moment Viona was satisfied. She had swept through all the guards and had not been questioned. With every second she was pulling farther and farther away from Earth, her destination—Uranus—still nothing more than a speck on the edge of the Solar System.

Her hands hovering over the control panel, Viona looked about her on to the vast deeps of space, then almost automatically she found herself looking at the enormous wedge of darkness which blotted out the more distant stars. She switched on the radio to Waveband 892 and waited for the response.

In Quorne's laboratory the Amazon gave the return signal. Abna went on working and listening at the same time as Viona's voice came through the speaker.

"I managed to get clear of the guards all right, so I should be safe from now on," Viona said, her words blurring now and again with solar static. "Right now I'm looking at the Smudge you mentioned. It's of enormous size and doesn't look very far away. Over,"

"Chart which stars are on its edge," the Amazon replied, "and then we can estimate its distance. Over."

There was a long interval, during which the Amazon returned to her work, then as Viona's voice came through again, the Amazon made notes. Viona gave a list of the required stars and the Amazon, knowing their distances by heart, gave a shrug.

"Neither nearer nor farther than it ought to be," she said. "My calculations on its speed must be correct. I was—"

She paused as Viona's voice came through, sharp with alarm.

"Mother, I'm being pursued!"

Abna looked up quickly, his eyes narrowed. The Amazon flashed him a glance, then looked back at the equipment.

"There are three vessels," Viona continued. "I can see them distinctly. They are a very long way off yet but I think they're gaining on me. Over."

"Since they must be Zanjian vessels, that's only to be expected," the Amazon replied. "Their dense bodies can withstand even the most brutal acceleration.... What weapons have you on that machine, Viona?"

Brief interval as the radio waves flashed across the void.

"Nothing very effective. Only a small protonic cannon and a couple of heat beams. Over."

"No use at all against those invading vessels...." The Amazon tapped her finger ends impatiently on the bench as she thought swiftly, then as her eyes travelled over the work upon which she and Abna had been engaged, she added quickly: "Put on all the speed you can endure. Do all you can to keep your distance from your followers, for if they reach you they will spare you no mercy. Report to me on your distance from Earth every sixty seconds."

The Amazon moved swiftly back to the tangle of wires, coils, and equipment, which were to be used for the energy projector.

"Only one way to save Viona," she said quickly. "We must assemble this material into a small projector, which I can carry, and give it an atom battery. The larger ones we had planned can come later. The immediate need is to save Viona and—"

"But wait a moment, Vi," Abna interrupted. "What do you imagine you can do? Look at the start Viona has, and we haven't even a spaceship here."

"I notice Quorne has duplicated my transportation-dissembly system," the Amazon said. "And incorporating a fourth-dimension mode, too. There's an identical instrument over there. One of the many secrets he stole from me."

"Abna frowned. "You mean—"

"I mean I must have a projector capable of wiping out these Zanjians—which this one will do—and then I must transmit myself to a point in space approximately where Viona is, which is why I want her distance to be given. I'll never be noticed as a single figure in the depths of space. With me I can take a recoil-gun which will pilot me about."

"And when you've taken such a risk, how do you propose to get inside the three vessels and deal with the Zanjians?"

"By the external safety lock which opens from the outside. There's one on every spaceship."

"One million miles...," came Viona's voice.

"I'll go with you," Abna said urgently, hurrying to get the projector components into order—but the Amazon shook her head.

"Two of us in space might be seen, Abna, especially since you are so much bigger than I am. Besides, we shall need this laboratory quite a deal yet to make larger projectors to deal with the Zanjians here on Earth. You'd better stay and go on making projectors, as well as guarding the place.... My only worry now is: has Quorne a spacesuit in this laboratory?"

The Amazon began to prowl around intently, opening cabinets and lockers, while Abna continued the assembly of a small projector. Then Viona's voice came again.

"Six million, five hundred and eighty thousand miles from Earth. Zanjians gaining slowly...."

The Amazon took one of four spacesuits from a metal cabinet and went across to Abna with it. She said:

"Viona is evidently travelling at half the speed of light now since she has covered over 5,000,000 miles in the last sixty seconds. It's not enough speed if she's to outdistance her pursuers—or even maintain her present distance from them."

CHAPTER TEN
NO LONGER INVINCIBLE

She turned to helping Abna with the assembly of the projector. At every minute, as she had been instructed, Viona gave her distance from Earth, and apparently she was not increasing her velocity. The Zanjians were still gaining.

Dawn was approaching and Viona reported herself well beyond the orbit of Mars, and her pursuers no more than 20,000,000 miles away before the projector was finished. The Amazon swallowed some of the restorative pills she always carried with her then. Refreshed, made her preparations while Abna checked over the atom-dissembly equipment.

"To warn you to take care of yourself, Vi, sounds silly," he said, "but perhaps there isn't any harm in saying it. I'll stay here and hope for the best. Viona will probably let me know by radio what is happening."

The Amazon nodded, and then screwed her helmet into position. Over her shoulder she slung the completed projector with its self-generating atom battery, and about her waist was the usual weapon-and-instrument belt supplied with all spacesuits. Thus prepared, she stepped into the area of the dissembly machine and waited for Viona's next distance reading.

It came at length, and Abna programmed the dissembly-machine for the required point. Then he shook the Amazon's gloved hand and activated the power.

She was fully prepared for the anguish which resulted, but that did not make it any the more endurable. The laboratory blotted out around her and there came the quiescence of dissolution. Then gradually that stirring of inner forces as the reassembly of her body, complete to the space suit and every material thing about her, began to take place. She opened her eyes and looked through her helmet-vizor on to the endless void.

She was not far from the region of the asteroids. A tiny speck, catching the glare of the sun, indicated the position of Viona's machine as it hurtled on its journey to Uranus. In the opposite direction, rapidly increasing in size, were three more specks. The Amazon smiled a little to herself, congratulating the computer back on Earth that had worked out her position for her. It had also imparted her a forward speed only slightly less than that of the approaching space machines. She weighed up the exact course the three pursuing machines were taking, then realizing she was perhaps 500 miles away from their path, she switched on the recoil gun and fired it between her enormous space boots. Immediately she was hurled forward as the recoil went backwards.

It was by no means the first time the Amazon had thus piloted herself about in weightless, non-resistant space, and once she had started moving forward, she kept on doing it at the same velocity since there was nothing to check her speed and no friction to slow her down. So, like a tiny bloated speck she drifted into the region the onrushing Zanjian machines would have to take, adjusting her position by gentle recoil bursts.

If, as she hoped, her timing was correct, she would be below the machines and therefore unlikely to be seen.

She waited, tensed. The three machines hurtled nearer, gradually overtaking her—then the foremost one shot over her with soundless velocity. Instantly the Amazon found herself swung violently towards the ship's mass attraction. The magnetic soles in her boots tilted upwards to the machine's metallic mass and she found herself anchored to the outer plates. To all normal standards she was head downward in space, but in an abyss with no up or down and the gravitation dragging from a central point everything, from her aspect, was the right way up.

Carefully, she began moving—carefully to avoid the sound of her heavy boots being transmitted through the plates to the air inside the machine. Gradually, as though she were walking a slowly turning floor, she came to the summit of the machine, keeping low down by the conning tower so that she would not be seen from the other vessel flying abreast. As she had expected, there was an emergency exterior lock and it was only the work of a moment for her to open it. She did so with infinite care, laying back the cover and peering into the empty chamber below. Beyond it was the door that led into the ship's interior, the gap between being essential so that no air could escape when the outer lock was opened.

She lowered herself into the cavity, closed the lock behind her, then felt around for the latch which would open the inner door. She found it with difficulty through her gloved hands. In normal circumstances she would have removed her suit, but there was always the chance the reverse mechanism on the dissembler would react and catch her unawares, in which case dissolution might take place in the void if she were not fully protected.

The latch slid over under her fingers and she opened the door a fraction of an inch, then a little further, until she could see three Zanjians seated at the control panel, intent on the course and the view of space in front of them. They were conversing with each other in their own language.

Carefully the Amazon unhitched the projector from about her shoulder, but by sheer misfortune it swung a little too far as she did so and caught the metal edge of the doorway. Instantly the three men glanced behind them in surprise. A fraction of a second elapsed while they absorbed the meaning of a figure in a spacesuit visible through the crack in the door—then one of them hurled himself forward.

The Amazon tried to shut the door quickly, but

that iron-hard body collided with it before she could complete the operation. Under its impact she went flying backwards and hit the wall, her resilient suit saving her from injury—and indeed rebounding her slightly.

In the split seconds which elapsed whilst the Zanjian looked about him in the gloom she sighted her projector and fired. The invisible energy struck the Zanjian as he hurtled toward her and stopped him in his tracks. He gasped, gave a convulsive shudder, then crashed on to his face and became still.

Delighted at the success of her weapon, the Amazon crept to the open doorway again. The two remaining men were looking in her direction, evidently waiting for their comrade to return. She fired instantly, wiping out the man on the right. The man on the left moved so rapidly that she could not get refocussed quickly enough. Reaching her, his steel-strong hands began to batter at the transparent casing of her helmet. With a tremendous effort she tore free and blundered into the control room. Immediately the Zanjian was after her, giving her no time to sight her gun.

She flung out her foot at the last second and the heavy metal boot crashed into the man's stomach, bringing him up short. Having gained the initial advantage, the Amazon tore at the metal chair beside her. It was welded to the floor but came free at the terrific twisting the Amazon gave it.

She whirled it over her head and smashed it down hard on the Zanjian's head as he slowly recovered his breath. Though the blow did not stun him, he staggered dizzily, and that was all the Amazon needed. It gave her time in which to sight her gun.

She fired. The man gasped, his hands clawing the air, then he went down and remained there. But he still moved a little, so evidently the energy had only struck him a glancing blow and he had not absorbed the full current. The Amazon raised her weapon to finish the job, then changed her mind as a thought struck her.

She switched on her audiophone and snapped: "Get up!"

It was some moments before the half-paralyzed creature had the strength to obey, and when he had done so, he rocked on his feet.

"Order the two other machines to stop the pursuit of that Earth space ship," the Amazon commanded. "Since this vessel is ahead of the others, it is obviously the leader. Hurry!"

The creature moved to the radio switchboard, the Amazon keeping him covered with the projector. He switched on the apparatus and jabbered a few words in his own tongue, which the Amazon was incapable of interpreting.

"Since I do not understand your language I'll wait and see if your order is carried out," she said.

"You have there a weapon which is capable of destroying us—the invincible ones," the creature remarked. "Such a thing has never happened in all our history. Do you think I would be fool enough to try to defy your instructions?"

"You might be. I'll stay and make sure in any case."

The creature raised and lowered his vast shoulders and then went to work on his own control panel, firing the forward rockets so that his own speed was slowed down. Beside him—the Amazon noted through the observation window—the other two vessels were checking their advance, too. Until, by slow degrees, they began to reach a relative standstill in space.

"You are more sensible than I thought," the Amazon commented. "Now you can tell me something else. Which of the weapons against the wall here is capable of penetrating the armor-hide of those space machines?"

Sensing what was in her mind, the Zanjian did not answer. She looked at him fixedly through her helmet visor and levelled her projector more directly.

"I asked you a question!" she snapped.

"And I am not answering it, Earth woman. You only wish to know so you can destroy my comrades."

"Can you give me any good reason why you should live—any of you? When you have invaded and enslaved my world?"

The Zanjian's only response was his customary stony glare. The Amazon gave a bitter smile, then her thumb pressed hard on the projector. It had always been her code to wipe out whatever antagonized her—and it had not changed with the years. This time, the Zanjian got the full blast of the mysterious energy, and he toppled slowly out of his chair and collapsed heavily on the metal floor.

Immediately the Amazon slung the projector back

on to her shoulder and looked at the weapons one by one, then at the vessels apparently motionless outside and awaiting fresh orders. In fact, to judge from the bobbing light on the communication panel, somebody was trying to get through.

Finally the Amazon selected a weapon at random, having no idea of its capabilities but looking workman-like enough. She found the control button and then set the prismatic sight in position so that it dead-centered the vessel on her left. Experimentally she pressed the button.

Space itself seemed to explode around her with shattering and yet noiseless violence. Not only did she completely destroy the vessel at which she had aimed, volatizing it into cosmic dust, but she also blew apart the vessel in which she was standing. Possibly it was caused by the furious recoil of the appalling energy she had used—or perhaps the gun was only intended to work on small outbursts instead of the entire energy-quota at one blast.

Whatever the causes, the Amazon found herself twirling head over heels in the gulf, surrounded by floating masses of ruptured metal and the bodies of the three Zanjians she had slain. The remaining vessel was broken into two ragged halves looking like two empty shells of an egg.

Gradually the Amazon's dizzying, twirling motion ceased, then she began to drift into the little whirlpool of metal fragments and dead Zanjians. Her task was complete and there was now nothing she could do but await the reverse action on the dissembler on faraway Earth that would return her to her starting point.

CHAPTER ELEVEN
UNDERGROUND RESISTANCE

Practically motionless in the midst of the drifting wreckage, she looked for Viona's ship but she failed to detect it. It was so small in comparison to the infinite it would demand instruments to determine its position, and then a telescope to see it. But she was able to observe the Dark—a vast, still far-distant curtain, which gave a curious, numbing depth to space in the region behind the nearest visible stars.

Looking at it, she realized with some regret how little progress she and Abna had made in solving its mystery. Even now the thought of relying on Sefian to overcome the problem did not fill her with any enthusiasm. It seemed to her more like a scientific enigma that it would take the cleverest trained scientists all their time to analyze.

Then the dissembler mechanism suddenly operated. She recognized the dragging pull at the molecules of her body. Space warped and vanished before her tortured gaze then she was being helped up from the floor by Abna in the laboratory from which she had started.

In a moment or two he had her helmet unscrewed and the spacesuit off. She sank into a chair, a little shaken from her ordeal, then drank the restorative that Abna gave her. Gradually, her tremendous strength overcame physical disabilities and she felt herself again.

"Well?" Abna asked anxiously. "Did you manage it?"

"With complete success," she responded, and gave him the details. "If any further pursuit is attempted, it will not be for some time and by then I fancy Viona will have reached Uranus and be able to keep out of harm's way."

"The trip took you three hours," Abna said, glancing at the clock. "I never had an easy moment, either."

The Amazon smiled a little. "I cannot see that you had any cause for worry, Abna. Surely, had anything happened to me, you are quite self-sufficient?"

He eyed her steadily as she rose to her feet, a half cynical light in her violet eyes.

"You may not realize it," he said, "but you are slowly drifting back to being the Golden Amazon I first knew—hard, cold, unyielding. Why do you have to do it?"

"I have come to realize, Abna, that though we are so closely associated, each of us has too strong an individuality to have it submerged by the other. Gradually things are settling down as they should be. We are becoming scientific partners—nothing more—the one outcome of our union being Viona, who is a mental product of both of us. With the powers we possess,

Abna, we are not as other human beings. I don't mean that in the egotistical sense. It's plain truth."

"I'm human enough, I'm afraid, to still believe a man can love a woman dearly—as I love you."

"Love me?" The Amazon raised an eyebrow. "When I asked you to stay beside me instead of chasing Viona into the Twenty-Fifth Plane, you refused. I knew then that your love is not so much for me as Viona. I'm not blaming you. I am simply pointing it out. So, if I decide to more or less fight my own battles with you just as my scientific partner you mustn't blame me."

Abna was silent for a long moment. When he spoke again he had changed the subject.

"There is a meal waiting in the house. I think we had better have it; then you'll need some sleep after your efforts. While you have been absent I've partly completed a giant energy projector on the lines of the small one. I gather from Viona that the wavelength is pretty devastating."

"Viona?" The Amazon glanced back over her shoulder.

"She kept in touch with me by radio. I learned you smashed those three enemy ships in pieces."

"True—but the projector was not responsible for that. It was one of the Zanjians' own weapons. However, the wavelength is certainly fatal. I proved that much."

The lounge had been reached and the Amazon and Abna moved over to where refreshment was waiting on the table.

"And you haven't been attacked?" the Amazon questioned.

"So far, no. I can only think of one reason. Since Viona's ship was sighted and pursued, it is probable that the Zanjian ruler imagined we were aboard it and so called off any further search.... Since the destruction of those pursuing machines will certainly be reported, I think we had better be on our guard from here on. The sooner the projector I'm working on is finished, the better for us."

* * * * * * *

One hour's rest was sufficient to restore the Amazon to normal, and after that she spent her time with Abna working in the laboratory and completed the giant version of the projector.

"Even if we are attacked," the Amazon said, "the smaller projector I used in space is still in order. That can give a good account of itself."

"Doubtless, but the greater the size, the bigger area of destruction we have."

They both became silent again, their minds on their work. To complete the task on which they were engaged would certainly take them the remainder of the day—as indeed it did, and longer.

It was not far from midnight when the big instrument was finished, a masterpiece of machine-tool creation and scientific engineering.

"One alone against the hordes of Zanji is by no means sufficient," the Amazon said. "We need them in the thousands, with thousands of planes to carry them, if we are to uproot these interlopers. This problem has gone beyond our little province here."

Abna nodded. "The same idea which occurred to me. I think our only course is to try to contact those men and women who have formed a resistance army underground. I gather from radio reports on secret wavebands that they are based somewhere in London. Our only chance is to go there, armed with this projector. Or, better still, with two projectors: this one, and the little one. We'll probably meet plenty of trouble on the way but—"

"No reason why we should," the Amazon intervened. "We can instantly transport ourselves to the middle of London as easily as to the most distant planet."

"Of course!" Abna smiled ruefully as he glanced toward the dissembly equipment. "I had forgotten all about that."

"We'll set it without the reverse mechanism," the Amazon added. "In that way we shall not be snatched back after a given interval. And," she added, with a glance at the clock, "there's no better time to start than now."

She picked up her small projector and Abna shouldered the larger one, walking with it to the transmission plate of the equipment. He had just arrived in position and the Amazon had taken her stand beside him when the outer laboratory door flew open. Out in the night, illuminated by the glare of the laboratory, were three Zanjians, their guns ready.

Instantly the Amazon snapped the dissembler

switch and for her and Abna the laboratory blanked out completely just as livid fire from the Zanjians' guns streaked toward them. The next thing they knew they were standing in the midst of London's ruins.

"Only just in time," Abna murmured. "Where do we go from here?"

"We start moving and destroy anybody who is not of this planet," the Amazon decided and commenced walking forward. "We're bound to contact somebody before long."

"And those Zanjians will be on the lookout for us, too, when those others we just escaped report back on our dissolution," Abna commented.

"Maybe. They had no idea where we went, remember."

Moving cautiously, they crept through the ruins until they came to a clear stretch where they could see a good deal of the shattered metropolis spread out in front of them. Lighting was patchy, but they could faintly see moving figures in the distance, too far away to be determined as either Zanjians or Earthlings.

The Amazon was on the verge of speaking when a slight sound to the rear caught her abnormally sharp hearing. She turned instantly and was just in time to see a dim figure creeping amid the shadows. As far as she could tell, it was too tall for a Zanjian. Immediately she leapt lithely through the debris, caught up with the figure, and swung him round by a grip on his shoulder.

It was a man in tattered shirt and trousers. He half began to drag away, then recognising the face and figure of the Amazon in the dim moonlight he gave a little gasp of relief.

"The Amazon!" he exclaimed. "Thank heaven! For the first time since these invaders came I feel really safe!"

"Who are you?" the Amazon questioned, as Abna came across to join them.

"Martin Daws by name. I used to be an engineer before all this happened. Amazon, where have you been for so long? The people have been looking for you, hoping you'd reappear among us to fight with us—"

"I am going to do just that," the Amazon said. "My husband and I had weapons to make before we dared to appear. These Zanjians are proof against ordinary means of attack."

"How well we know that," Martin Daws muttered.

"We?" the Amazon questioned. "You mean you are one of the resistance army?"

"Certainly I am. There isn't a man or woman in the world who isn't, providing they are free enough to move around—as I am. I have just been looking for some more stray men and women to add to our numbers."

"Where are your headquarters?" Abna asked.

Martin Daws jerked his head. "This way. And be prepared for attack. These invaders are everywhere."

The Amazon and Abna followed closely behind him as he picked his way through the ruins until he gained a big manhole cover.

"Sewers?" Abna questioned.

"No. We're occupying the air-conditioning chambers under the city. As you know, they are of enormous size and used for keeping the city atmosphere at an equable purity—"

Martin Daws broke off and simultaneously the Amazon jabbed the button her projector. With her keen night sight she had observed the silent approach of three squat figures with enormously wide shoulders—three Zanjians who had evidently been on the watch for Daws' return. Before they could fire their weapons, the projector's fatal energy dropped them in their tracks.

"There may be others," Daws said, his voice indicating his astonishment at the efficiency of the Amazon's weapon. "Let's get below."

He seized the manhole cover ring and pulled on it with all his strength, struggling to lift the heavy iron lid. Then the Amazon motioned him away, locked her fingers round the ring and pulled the three-inch thick cover up without effort. Below, an iron ladder was revealed going down into the darkness.

Daws went first and Abna last. He heaved the cover back into place and then felt his way down to the limit of the ladder. Near him he could hear the engineer and the Amazon breathing.

"This way," Daws said, catching at the Amazon's arm—and with Abna hanging on to her they moved through the pitch dark of an underground tunnel until far away a light appeared like a star. It grew larger and at last revealed itself as the entrance to one of the colossal air-conditioning plant chambers that had been built under the city in the last few years. Here the Amazon paused, gazing around her in the glow of the yellow tinted safety lamps upon thousands of men and women, most of them grouped into families, having with them what few possessions they had managed to snatch in their escape below.

"Two more chambers beyond this one are filled with people," Daws explained.

"That's good," the Amazon responded, her violet eyes bright. "Here is an army which only needs weapons. And these it shall have in good time."

She began moving quickly, finally selecting one of the silent generating plants as her platform and standing upon it.

"People, do you not recognise me?" she cried, her voice echoing through the great space.

Immediately the men and women looked in her direction—and a cry went up.

"The Golden Amazon!"

"And Abna," somebody added.

The Amazon held up her hand for silence.

"One of your number led me here," she said. "Martin Daws by name. I have come amongst you again with the sole objective of overthrowing these usurpers who have taken possession of our planet."

"Only you and Abna can defeat the invaders!" Daws insisted, in the front of the crowd. "You have only to command us and we'll follow."

"Very well then." The Amazon turned to the projector Abna was carrying on his shoulder. "I am giving you all a pretty difficult task, but it is the only way we can gain victory. Here is a projector wired exactly to produce an energy wave capable of destroying the invaders. We need thousands like it, and a fleet of planes to carry the projectors. Everything must be so arranged that we can strike at a given moment and launch a devastating onslaught which will leave these beings reeling and unable to recover."

The people glanced at one another, then Daws said, "We have no engineering resources down here, Amazon."

"I know," she responded. "That is why I said the problem would be difficult. But we can do it."

"And the Zanjians have full control over all sources of power, metals, and everything else," Daws added. "I do not see there is anything we can do."

"These air-conditioning chambers extend under the whole city, including the engineering sections," she said. "We must find a way in from below to gain the necessary machine tools. And we will. I want ten men and women to act as my subordinates and with them I will now discuss our plans."

The Amazon left her perch and walked over to the quietest corner of the vast space that she could find, Abna close behind her. After a while the ten men and women for whom she had asked had sorted themselves out to join her. All of them looked capable and intelligent.

"There is no map handy of this underworld," the Amazon told them, "but as I had a hand in the design, I know from memory the exact layout—which is like this...."

CHAPTER TWELVE
KRON MEETS HIS SUPERIOR

The Amazon removed an ordinary raygun from her belt, narrowed the firing nozzle down to its smallest aperture and then proceeded to trace on the metal wall a rough map. It took her ten minutes, but at the end of the time every important part, together with its approximate distance, had been included.

"You will notice," she said, putting the gun away, "that we are connected to all these engineering centers by the tunnels which lead from this purifying chamber. Abna and I both have paralyzing guns with us. They are powerful enough to stop the activities of the Zanjians for a while—long enough for us to appropriate machine tools anyway, and these rayguns are penetrating enough to eat through a tunnel ceiling—the floor of whichever place we decide to attack—in a matter of seconds. The big energy projector is too large to carry, and the little one not large enough to take care of a lot of enemies in quick succession. Best to use the paralyzers."

"Then what are we waiting for?" Martin Daws asked. "I suggest we should go into action immediately. I have discovered that during the night the guard is not as heavy in the daytime."

"Then we'll try," the Amazon decided, "and to begin with we had better go as a small party. If the prospect is favourable, we will need considerable numbers of us to get the necessary equipment moved.... Come."

She began to lead he way with Abna beside her, and once she had gathered her bearings after leaving the central chamber, she moved rapidly down the dimly lighted circular tunnels with their smooth metal walls through which blew soft warm air. All the time she and those to the rear who had become her lieutenants hurried onwards, they could detect the muffled rumbling of machinery, partly from the power houses restarted in the heart of the battered city, and partly from the air-purifying pumps. Then, presently, the Amazon began to slow down, studying the curved ceiling above her. Presently she stopped entirely and indicated a small, thickly barred grating.

"According to my calculations we are now directly under the first machine-tool factory," she said. "Abna, raise me to the grating."

He lifted her, and hooking her fingers into the metal holes she angled her face sideways and could get a slantwise view of machinery and two of the men of Zanji going back and forth.

"Keep hold of me," she whispered to Abna, and he obeyed, apparently finding her weight no effort to hold aloft.

She pulled her raygun from her belt and, it still being

on the narrowest aperture, she set the needle of searing flame to bite through the edges of the grille above her. In less than ten seconds the last piece gave way and she caught it deftly. Then she gripped bold of the edge of the aperture and muscled herself up, peering cautiously around.

For the moment all was safe. The Zanjians, in their perambulating watch ever the equipment, had travelled to the far end of the huge room. So she hauled herself up the remaining distance, motioned quickly fur Abna to follow, and then fled crouchingly for the safety of the nearest machine.

Using the machines for cover, she made her way quickly to the farther end of the machine-room, Abna not far behind her, until she had reached a point where she was only a few feet from two of the stunted, powerful Zanjians.

"Are you going to deal with them or shall I?" Abna murmured.

"I will." The Amazon had her paralyzer in her hand. "There are probably others somewhere: see if you can locate them."

Abna nodded and glided away. The Amazon sighted her paralyzer carefully and pressed the button. Instead of operating, however, it buzzed sharply and only emitted a thin stream of acrid smoke. Somehow the delicate firing mechanism had become damaged, or else misplaced through atomic dissembly.

From such close quarters the Zanjians could not help but hear the buzzing of the faulty instrument, and they swung in time to see the Amazon dodge back from sight. Immediately their own weapons were in their hands and they were pounding towards her. She gave a desperate glance about her and then took a flying leap with all the power of her leg muscles. It lifted her easily to the top of the motionless machine tool equipment nearby, across which was a parallel bar.

Her hands clutched it and at the same time she spun round with an agility that would have done credit to any trapeze performer. Simultaneously her feet shot out, each foot timed that it struck one of the Zanjians in the face. They were uninjured, but their aim was deflected. Releasing the bar, she flew over their heads, dropped, leaped again, and then ran for her life down a short aisle. The pounding of mighty weights came behind her and a vicious jet of fire ripped a fissure in the metal of a machine close beside her.

Then as the sound of the concussive footfalls stopped, she twirled round, watching the amazing sight of Abna trying to grapple with both Zanjians at once. He had evidently approached from the side and had not had time to draw his own paralyzer. He had the head of each Zanjian imprisoned under his arms and he was hanging on desperately.

That he must lose such a struggle was obvious— but the instant she realized the situation, the Amazon hurtled back down the aisle, snatched Abna's paralyzer from his belt, and then fired it at each Zanjian in turn. Rigid, in exactly the position they had been while Abna had held them, they dropped to the floor.

"That was close," Abna said. "But these are the only guards in the place. I'd just finished checking on that when I heard them on the move and came to investigate. I've locked the door."

"Good." The Amazon glanced around her quickly. "It's possible we shan't be disturbed for some time."

She hurried back to the smashed grating and looked down on Martin Daws and the rest of the men in the tunnel below.

"Get all the help you can," she ordered. "There is heavy equipment and a generating plant to be moved. Hurry! Every second counts."

Daws and his colleagues nodded promptly and streaked away down the tunnel. The Amazon turned her attention back to the tool rack, selected the necessary tools for dismantling, and then with Abna went to work on the first machine that would have to be manhandled below in sections when the grating gap had been burned wider for the purpose.

That the Amazon had started something that would bring the wrath of the Zanjians down on her head she knew full well, but that did not deter her.

Working through the night, during which time the paralysis remained upon the Zanjians, some 200 of the strongest men moved all the necessary self-powered equipment under the Amazon's directions, transferring it to the main conditioning chamber and there reassembling it. By dawn all the necessary equipment had been obtained for turning out endless numbers of projectors, one of the machines in particular being capable of making metal by transposing the atoms of the air itself into solid matter. The process lowered the air pressure for a time, but since this was the spot where air-conditioning itself was taken care of, there was no hardship.

The following morning, Kron heard of the audacious seizure of the machine tools and immediately sent all the men he could spare to defeat the underground plot.

But by the time the first Zanjians invaded the underground the first fifty projectors were also coming off the assembly line, with the result that every Zanjian was wiped out the instant they set foot beyond the shattered door. Then the Amazon herself operated the metal-creating machine and created a new door, adding to it layer upon layer of metal to make it shock-proof. Then she left men standing by the projectors and went on with her work.

The second wave of Zanjians failed to get beyond the barrier. Then Kron sent out fliers to rain bombs down on the air-conditioning chambers. But here again he was foiled, as the great depth of the chambers stopped the explosions reaching them. Certainly there were moments when the Amazon and Abna looked anxiously above at the mighty braced dome of ceiling, but though the whole great space seemed to swing under the terrific concussions, it remained undamaged. When it had been built it had been specially prepared against possible onslaughts either by man or from space, and it came through the test with honours.

For the time being Kron stopped attacking, and the

Amazon and her colleagues continued working steadily. When 2,000 projectors had been made—every one of them patterned from the giant one Abna had built—the machine patterners were changed and small bullet-nosed wingless planes were made, designed to hold a pilot and a weapon controller.

The chief weapon was the energy-beam projector, with subsidiary weapons of heat-rays, proton guns, and disintegrators, though whether any of them would be of any use against the Zanjian machines was doubtful.

Kron launched an attack with another type of explosive, which succeeded in cracking the roof of the giant chamber. Possibly, had the attack been maintained, the entire machine-room might have collapsed, but evidently failure was again considered to be the result, so the attack was withdrawn.

The Amazon made use of the fissured roof and with powerful proton guns awaiting mounting within the fliers she widened the gap and drove a tunnel upwards, just wide enough to permit of the passage of one of the fliers, providing it was skilfully flown.

"In twelve more hours," she told Abna when her roof-widening activity was over, "we shall have 2,000 fliers ready for departure, and 4,000 men and women to man them. In the interval this gap in the roof must be kept clear at all costs."

"I'll guard it myself," Abna said, setting up a detector that would immediately show the approach of any person or flier when it was still a mile away.

Yet his guardianship was not necessary. Kron was

quite convinced that attack had failed and in consequence the tunnel to below was not detected.... But
he had men and fliers ready in case a sudden attack
was made. Even he, though, had not expected that the
resources below would be capable of putting 2,000
super-fast fighter-bombers in the air.

Just after dawn he received warning that a contin-
uous stream of machines was hurtling to the upper air,
and he immediately gave the order to attack. But the
two-man fliers were able to escape to get out in full
numbers before the Zanjian machines could get into
formation.

CHAPTER THIRTEEN
SCIENTIFIC GUINEA PIGS

As the Amazon, in her leading machine, with Abna piloting, twirled over the sunlit city, she operated the energy-projector, which had its nose flush with a trap in the floor. Its range was capable of reaching to the ground, and everywhere it swept it was like an invisible scythe of death, as far as Zanjians were concerned. Wherever they moved and the energy caught them they staggered and died. Nor were buildings any protection for them for the energy passed through solids easily. Yet normal Earth people were not affected, the energy being quite harmless to their constitution.

Half of the 2,000 fliers streaked to the west, heading for the other side of the world to deal with the Zanjian menace. Immediately they were pursued by the interlopers' machines and both sides became engaged in a crossfire of heat-beams and disintegrators—but manoeuvrability seemed to be the answer, for the smallness of the Amazon's machines made them capable of dodging and twisting with bewildering rapidity.

The energy beams took their toll, even through the armour-plated walls of the invaders' vessels. Above

London machine after machine went down and the energy-beams continued to play over the city. All day long the struggle raged, but it was obvious there could only be one end to it. When the last Zanjian attacker had been swept out of the sky, the Amazon gave the order to ground and what were left of her gallant band began to drift down toward the spaceport. It still stood intact, since in this battle no explosive had been used.

It was mid-evening when the last recalled flier returned to the London base, and by this time the Amazon was in the normal London headquarters, reestablishing contact with the recognized head of the state. With his advisers, all of whom had emerged from hiding on receiving the all-clear signal, he sat at the long table in the main cabinet room. With the Amazon and Abna, there were twenty men and women present.

"To say that we are grateful, Miss Brant, for your intervention in what could have been a tyrannical rule, sounds paltry," the head of the state said. "But you have my assurances that we are—deeply. Without you and Abna, and the very gallant men and women who helped you we—"

"Quite so," the Amazon intervened. "I do not need credit—or want it. I set out to destroy the Zanjians, and have done it. Technically the victory is my daughter's, since she provided the key for the energy that brought these interlopers to the dust.... I would suggest that you restore order as quickly as possible and make arrangements for the bodies of the dead to be incinerated. After that, see to your defences."

"Defences?" one of the ministers asked in surprise. "But surely we have gained victory?"

"Over the Zanjians, yes." The Amazon's face was grim. "It is possible there may yet be other invasions— even several of them. Our late lamented enemies only came here because the Dark out in space drove them to it. They chose our world as the nearest possibility to their own. Obviously, as the dark tide advances other planets may spew forth their inhabitants who might settle here. It depends how many of the planets are inhabited, and whether this world is suitable for the inhabitants of those planets. However, that is mere speculation. Abna and I have no time to deal with civic matters or the rearrangements of peoples. Our whole attention henceforth will be concentrated on trying once more to find a way to save Earth from the Dark when it comes. My next endeavor is to find Sefner Quorne."

The head of the state said: "Sefner Quorne is dead!"

The Amazon gave a start and a quick glance at Abna.

"Dead? But are you certain?"

"I ought to be. After Quorne had been slain, I was ordered to Kron's headquarters—in this very building—and told to take his place, chiefly as a person able to supply information about this planet. I refused, and was condemned to death. Fortunately, my aide rescued me and we escaped and fled underground.... However, there is no doubt that Quorne is dead. Kron told me so, and he certainly would not have sent for me if he could have had the much more compliant

Quorne."

"I see...." The Amazon sat thinking for a moment.

"Which puts a different complexion on things," Abna said, rising.

The Amazon nodded and rose, glancing at the head of the State as she did so.

"Should you require me for anything vital—not otherwise—use wavelength 402. I'm returning to my own home, with Abna, and granted a little peace we might be able to make some progress in the laboratory."

"Very well, Miss Brant. And thank you both again for all you have done."

The Amazon and Abna found their home and the laboratory still intact, but the Zanjian whom they had paralyzed had disappeared, evidently having recovered and joined his own fellows.

A meal and two hours rest came first, then the Amazon and Abna moved into the laboratory and began work.

Computations revealed the tremendous increase in the area of Dark, which was blotting out most of the further stars and was spread in a terrifying abyss of nothing to nearly all the northern celestial hemisphere.

"I think," Abna said at length, "we'll only perhaps gain some idea of how to defeat it by going into it and investigating its properties at first hand. Our instruments, powerful and sensitive though they are, do not tell us enough at this distance."

"Do you think we dare?" the Amazon asked. "It

registers zero. No heat, no light, no anything. I would have risked it long ago only I was afraid—and still am—that I might never emerge."

Abna turned aside and began to study the readings that had been made of the mystery area.

"No light or radiation conductivity. Complete lack of space-time medium.... That means that if we fly into it we shall not be able to have any lights or heat within our ship. To wear spacesuits would not help since the warmth inside them would be unavailable, there being nothing to carry it."

"Like flying straight into the tomb," the Amazon said, with a glance back to the telescopic mirror. "Nothing that lives or breathes as we do can survive where there is no air, no warmth, and no light. And we have no means of protection."

"There is one means," Abna said. "Adaptability—linked to mind over matter. With the correct mental application, the human frame is capable of being adapted to any known condition. There is no reason why you and I, by gradual stages, cannot accustom ourselves to almost unlimited periods when we can live without air, light, or heat and yet keep possession of our senses. That is the only way we can ever fly into the Dark, investigate it, and yet emerge again."

The Amazon frowned. "I don't doubt you could do it, Abna. But I simply don't possess your degree of mind over matter—"

Abna smiled. "Your ability is there, but dormant. The adaptability process will help it to develop—and

I'll be right alongside to help you, if need be."

"Very well—I'm willing to risk it," the Amazon agreed. "But surely the ship will not be capable of being piloted, because the energy cannot be transferred to the firing chambers without ether to carry it?"

"We must work out what space pilots call a boomerang course. We drive our vessel into the Dark at such an orbit that it presently turns, and, in a wide curve, goes back the way it came in—all from the initial velocity. In that way we would automatically come out into normal space once more."

The Amazon nodded quickly. "You have it, Abna. We'll need the *Ultra*, geared to travel several times faster than light by utilizing the fourth dimension, which foreshortens space. You work out the kind of instruments we need to adapt ourselves, and I'll have the computer devise a foolproof track into and out of the Dark."

Each with their particular task to do, they set to work. The Amazon had the easiest job since the computer did more or less everything for her. At the end of half an hour she had a course mapped out, which according to the figures, would cause the *Ultra* to hurtle into the Dark on a constant curve, gradually turning as it advanced. Then, without any loss in velocity, it would emerge from the Dark again almost at its starting point, the actual speed having to be well in excess of that of light in order to emerge ahead of the advancing Dark.

Abna, for his part, listened to the Amazon's mathematical explanations detachedly, his mind chiefly centered on the construction of a special plant for producing adaptability. The final answer was that he began to create metal plates with an air-to-matter machine and, in a corner of the laboratory, Abna created a sealed chamber large enough to hold himself, the Amazon, and all the necessary instruments. On the outer side of the plates he added an insulating material of his own design which, for once, had the highly scientific Amazon completely baffled.

"What is it?" she questioned.

"It is composed of triply interlocked atoms which, when electrically excited, will eliminate all space-time within this chamber, producing conditions exactly the same as those in the Dark area."

"Then if we can eliminate space-time in this fashion, and seal it off from the rest of the laboratory, why can't we line our space machine that way? In that way we'd be a space-time shell inside non-space."

"We could do it, but how can we be in sympathy with the vacuum if we seal ourselves from it? We have to be in it and of it to get the results we want. We want both our physical reactions to it while the instruments register in stopwatch fashion all the other points we want to know. We have to be part of the conditions, Vi, to ever get within grasping distance of understanding them."

Satisfied on this point, the Amazon turned her attention to helping, and throughout the night she and Abna manufactured the necessary instruments. By dawn they were finished and housed within the 'conditioning chamber'.

"Obviously," Abna said, after he had checked the instruments, "we shall not be able to suddenly make ourselves adaptable to non-space. It will have to be done by easy stages.... So let's try the first effort. In case either of us finds the strain getting too much and cannot communicate because of lack of air or contact with each other, I have devised an automatic system which will cut out the instruments."

He indicated them, and then the chairs screwed to the floor in the center of the chamber. The Amazon sat in one, her yellow hands on the alarm switch, and Abna took the other. Before him was the main keyboard, and a lever movement closed the insulated shield across the entrance lock. The light above remained on, but if everything went according to plan it would gradually disappear as spatial dark and cold descended.

"Instruments will show just how much we have been able to stand," he remarked. "So, Vi, are you ready?"

"Yes," she answered, her beautiful features set in a hard, resolute mould.

"Never afraid to take a chance, are you?" Abna murmured, reverting for a moment to his normal, happy-go-lucky self. "All right—here it is."

He shifted the control switch, and outside the chamber, the necessary power engines went into action, distorting and absorbing the fabric of space-time from the chamber by electrical processes. The Amazon felt the effect first at her extremities. Her feet and hands went dead so that she had no consciousness of toes or fingers.

She turned her head to look at Abna. His powerful face was strained, but button by button he stepped up the voltage and the deadening effect of increasing cold and decreasing power of sensation continued. The Amazon began to feel her heart pounding as her breathing became labored.

CHAPTER FOURTEEN
MESSAGE FROM BRODIX

After a while, which seemed like an eternity to the Amazon—for all her great strength—the light above began to become dimmer, filling the chamber with sinister, densely black shadows. This gradual descent into the no-world of non-space-time had something incredibly horrifying about it, so completely was it divorced from all natural things.

At last, before the light had entirely gone, the Amazon realized that she could not breathe, that her heart was doing its utmost to burst—she imagined she moved her dead fingers but could not be sure.

Instantly light returned and with it a draft of air. She sank back in her chair near fainting, trickles of perspiration running down her face. Abna too looked as if he had just emerged from a Turkish bath, his hair matted to his head.

"That's more than enough for the first time," he said, looking at the instruments. "At least we managed to stand the effect in half its actual strength—and for nearly two minutes. We must keep on doing it, for longer and longer periods, until finally we can tolerate it for an hour or more without losing consciousness."

The Amazon nodded slowly, straightening up again. Abna pulled the lever that opened the door slide and fresh sir came surging into the pressure-lowered chamber. Feeling more dead then alive, the Amazon crawled out into the laboratory with Abna behind her. They spent a while recovering their scattered wits, then the Amazon frowned.

"I wonder why we don't receive any messages from Viona?"

Abna shrugged. "She's exploring, I suppose, and since she knows all pursuit was destroyed I should imagine she doesn't consider communication is necessary."

"I hope you're right," the Amazon responded anxiously.

For half an hour they rested, then once again they walked into the 'conditioning chamber' and put themselves through their ordeal. To their satisfaction they extended their time on this occasion by ten minutes before giving in, and they also held on long enough for the light to completely vanish, so that in effect they were actually almost at the same conditions as those existing in non-space-time.

And this was only the commencement of their efforts at adaptation. For many days they experimented, until at the end of a fortnight they found themselves able to remain for an hour in total darkness and utter silence, unaware of each other, unable to feel anything and yet with their minds alert.

"I think," Abna said, when this final test had been made and he was satisfied with their bodily reactions afterwards, "that we are conditioned enough to make the trip, Vi. Though some time will elapse before we reach the Dark, that will not make us any the less adaptable when we fly into it."

"That being the case, I must discover if the *Ultra* is still at the spaceport where I left it," the Amazon said. "My ship has its own protective screens, so it should be safe," she added, before hurrying from the laboratory to change into normal attire for a quick visit to London. It took her ten minutes to get there by her fast atom helicoplane.

The *Ultra* was safe in the spaceport where she had left it, and loading and provisioning was soon accomplished. Then at sunset the mighty machine leaped skyward, hurtling with ever mounting speed into the sky, until sit last the sky itself had gone and there was only the familiar void with the far distant backdrop where a V-shaped wedge blanked out stars and nebulae.

"I feel like making a detour to Uranus to see if we can find Viona," the Amazon said, considering the green planet in the remote depths.

"I'm as anxious as you are to establish contact with her again," Abna answered, "but I think it would be more sensible to first complete the business on which we've embarked. Unless we discover something in the Dark which demands great urgency, we can call at Uranus on our return trip."

The Amazon nodded and let the decision rest at

that. She gave a glance back at Earth, out to the murky distances where lay the Dark, and then moved the complicated controls on the matrix which controlled the enigmatic fourth-dimensional equipment

Immediately the *Ultra* was blanked out from the normal space and rotated through a mathematical angle in much the same way as a rolling object might change its base to its top in a single motion. So it happened here, with the difference that the *Ultra*, in a few brief seconds, bridged countless millions of miles whilst moving through a dimensional space telescoped in relation to the normal void. The vessel emerged from the hyperspace some 230-million miles beyond Pluto, which brought the Dark considerably nearer, though on terms of distance it was still vastly far away. Just how far away, the Amazon was at that moment trying to figure out. Beside her Abna waited patiently for the results of her calculations.

"We'll need eighteen more leaps like that before we come within measurable distance of our goal," the Amazon announced finally. "So we'd better take it gradually. Cruise for awhile in free space—as now; make another fourth dimensional leap; cruise again, and so on."

Abna nodded. "That being the case, I'll take the first spell at the controls, while you fix something to eat."

So, faster and faster, the *Ultra* hurtled through the immeasurable reaches of space. Since the journey was being made in foreshortened leaps, there was no necessity in the normal intervals to achieve maximum velocity—but just the same the machine kept on accelerating, but at a gentle pace whereby the inertia strain could be tolerated.

Then after a meal came another leap—which left the entire Solar System so far away it could hardly be seen, the sun having decreased to the size of a tenth-magnitude star. Then, nearly two weeks after the departure from Earth, the *Ultra* was only twenty-five-million miles from the charted edge of the cosmic fault. The view ahead was awe-inspiring. Not a light, a nebula, nor a single star. Nothing but the everlasting Dark, V-shaped to a point, its wider edge devouring the stars even as it was watched.

"Much more impressive than in our testing chamber," Abna remarked dubiously, studying it. "I only hope our calculations prove correct."

"Soon find out," the Amazon said. "I'm just setting our boomerang course. After that, we can only wait until we're inside the Dark."

"Which will take twenty minutes," Abna added glancing at the instruments.

The Amazon finished setting the course and then sat back in the control chair. Abna settled down at her side and closed his big hand over her yellow fingers as they lay on the switches, poised to re-activate the hyper-drive.

Immediately her violet eyes sought his inquiringly.

He murmured: "We've got beyond the sentimental stage, both of us. You said so yourself. Maybe a handclasp is sufficient goodbye."

The Amazon hesitated, then before she could decide what to do Abna had kissed her full on the mouth.

He said: "A husband is entitled to do that to his wife, and it may be the last chance I'll have. You may believe in this scientific partners business, but I don't. You may be the most perfect woman the Universe has ever known; I may be the only man with godlike powers when I choose to use them. But I still prefer to think we're human enough to be man and wife with a daughter somewhere on Uranus."

"We hope," the Amazon muttered. Then so she would not have to answer Abna's 'human' outburst, she turned her attention once more to the Dark. It was sweeping nearer, seeming to devour the Universe.

An instrument display flickered steadily, marking off the flying minutes and seconds. As the distance narrowed, the tension became too great for words. Abna's hand had returned to the Amazon's fingers and his hold tightened a little as the last millions of miles ran out—mere hops at the *Ultra*'s stupendous velocity.

Then with devastating suddenness, everything was gone. Light was extinguished. Air ceased. The Amazon and Abna were utterly motionless, not breathing, nor even conscious of their hearts. The vessel itself was presumably still moving in hyperspace through this utterly stagnant wilderness of Nothing. But of these things the Amazon and Abna were not conscious. Their minds were still active and they assumed the instruments were still recording everything, but deep down they were wondering if death would not be the answer to this plunge into the Incomprehensible.

Then both of them became conscious of something different. A stirring in their minds, some kind of mental vibration reaching them out of the quiescence....

Tarnec Brodix.... Tarnec Brodix....

The thought form took conceivable shape and assumed meaning. The name of the Mind of Minds— the greatest mathematician with whom the Amazon and Abna had ever came into contact. Tarnec Brodix, of a mathematical planet beyond the Universe.

Then, abruptly, like a picture brought into clear focus by the adjustment of a lens, he became intelligible, but even so he was not speaking in words but in thought-vibrations. This seemed contradictory to the Amazon at least, since there was nothing present to carry even a thought. Nonetheless her mind was attuned.

"Tarnec Brodix is communicating with you—but not the being you knew of the fleshly form. I exist now only as a mathematical variant, stripped of the powers I formerly possessed. I am being punished for a ghastly mistake I made in my calculations.... By one trivial error I dissolved my world and all that existed upon it. I, Tarnec Brodix, miscalculated!"

He went on: "You are receiving my thoughts through non-space-time because they are coming to you in mathematical form and even in non-space mathematics make sense because out of non-space mathematics originally formed the Universe. The fractional fault I created spread outwards from my Universe to encompass yours, which is why you now see an ever-growing area of utter Nothingness. However, at the moment of dissolution I did my utmost to transfer all my knowledge to a being somewhere in your own Universe, who would have the power of understanding the information I had conveyed. I found this brain in the Twenty-Fifth Plane of your Universe. I have since come to know that the brain belongs to Sefian Quorne."

The incredible mind of Brodix ceased communicating for a spell, and the motionless Amazon and Abna waited for what would happen next. Brilliant though both of them were, they found the conceptions of Brodix so colossal they could only vaguely grasp at the truth. Apparently, as near as their own minds could interpret it, Brodix had parted with most of his knowledge to a brain capable of receiving it, and the only brain available had proved to be none other than that of the still extremely young Sefian Quorne.

Then, presently, Brodix resumed: "To have handed on most of my knowledge and then not allow the recipient free scope to use it was obviously absurd—yet in the Twenty-Fifth Plane that was the position. So I gave him the necessary stimulus—mentally—to devise a way out of that plane and into the normal world to which he belonged. Because of that integrals were cancelled, and Sefian, his mother, Abna, and Sefner Quorne, his father, all came back to a common starting point."

He paused. The Amazon was feeling that she could not last out much longer. If only the *Ultra* would fly out of the Dark once more, then perhaps—

"In the mind of Sefian," Brodix continued, "there lies the answer to this Dark. He alone can overcome it by using the knowledge I have handed on to him. Sefian alone can do that and restore me to normal, as well as defeating the Dark. You must make him concentrate. If he does, he will find all the knowledge he needs deep within his brain, his physical age being of no consequence."

Brodix's thoughts were fading, and after a moment or two it became apparent why—for abruptly the *Ultra* sailed out of the Dark, hurtling back along the course on which it had entered the weird area, and life began to return to the two who had ventured into the abyss.

With a tremendous effort the Amazon, who alone understood the complications of the switchboard, dragged herself forward and fumbled around with the power switches. She snapped one sharply, which immediately killed the terrific acceleration. Constant velocity was in being, but because all increase in it had ceased, there was weightlessness. She found herself rising from the floor until, using the handrail, she dragged herself down again.

Abna, completely recovered, looked at her questioningly. Both of them were drawn and strained from their ordeal, and not a little incredulous.

CHAPTER FIFTEEN
DEADLY, FRIENDLESS PLANET

"Well," Abna said, "we certainly learned something!"

"More than expected," the Amazon admitted, glancing back toward the darkness across the star-dusted wastes. "Our grandson, it would appear, is a genius because Tarnec Brodix made him so. I am not sure whether I like it or not."

Abna frowned. "Not sure? What more could one ask for?"

"A great deal more, I think. And so, I imagine, will Viona when she knows. I do not think it is desirable or even pleasant to have had supreme genius wished on you by an utterly sexless creature who is nothing but an extraction of mathematical essences! I am remembering," the Amazon finished, her face hardening, "what the meddling of science did for me! And now it has apparently done the same thing for Sefian."

"Silly of me, I suppose," Abna murmured, "but I am quite at a loss."

"I mean that but for science I would have been a normal woman and not the scientific mistress of a system who has no real claims to being a woman at all. Sefian will never be a man in the true sense of the word. He will be a reincarnation of Tarnec Brodix, his own evolving personality completely eliminated. Viona will have to be told. At least we know that Sefian, with sufficient stimulus, should be able to save us from the Dark. We must find Viona on Uranus."

With a sigh the Amazon turned aside to the four-dimensional controls, and in a moment or two the vessel was making the first of its many transitions through telescoped space. In the normal intervals a meal was eaten and each took it in turn to rest. Then after the eighteenth leap through hyperspace, they found themselves within measurable distance of the known Solar System, once more with dense little Pluto not so very far away, with Neptune and Uranus behind him.

The Amazon slowed down the vessel's terrific speed somewhat and after that it was merely a matter of waiting as the millions of miles were eaten up.... Neptune and Pluto were finally to the rear with only green Uranus ahead, his surface masked—as were those of all the outer planets except Pluto—by densely whirling cloudbanks stirred by monstrous disturbances beneath.

"The more I look at that planet," Abna muttered, "the more I wonder if we shall ever find Viona alive. We were fools to let her go."

"There was no way of stopping her, Abna. She has too much of you and me in her for that."

Abna turned aside and studied the instruments, then

he gave a frown.

He said: "Uranus' atmosphere is almost pure nitric acid gas! I thought Jupiter and Saturn were bad enough with their ammoniated hydrogen envelopes, but this is considerably worse. There will not be a metal or a fabric which can withstand an atmosphere like that."

"Viona must have known that," the Amazon muttered. "Her own instruments would tell her. Perhaps she never landed here at all. If not, why couldn't she say so?"

"Whatever happens, we have to try and find her," Abna said.

They were both thinking the same thing—that when they plunged into this acid-gas atmosphere they would be taking one of the biggest risks since plunging into the Dark. The intense acid might even rot away the plates of the *Ultra*, and any spark from the exhaust tubes might equally cause a devastating explosion.

"Try the radio," the Amazon said.

Abna settled before the instrument, but though he repeatedly sent out a call-signal—which could be heard anywhere at full strength within forty million miles there being no solar static at this distance from the luminary—he received no answer. Then just as he had reached the end of his efforts the *Ultra* plunged with steadily slackening speed into the outermost edge of the deadly vapours.

Immediately the view outside vanished. There was only the swirling mystery of green, but it was so intensely poisonous that its contact with the great observation window produced speckling on the shock-proof glass.

"Turn back, Vi," Abna urged. "Viona would never have come to a world like this. It's obviously one which will be forever derelict—as far as our type of life is concerned, anyway."

"I'll have to finish what I've started," the Amazon answered, and kept her eyes on the screens as she took the vessel lower and lower through the obliterating reek.

Abna kept his eyes on the instruments. They registered Uranus' density as about the same as Earth, but the temperature was similar to that of Jupiter and Saturn, almost at the absolute zero of outer space. A more deadly, friendless world than far distant Uranus could hardly be imagined.

Then suddenly the Amazon swept the *Ultra* upwards. Just in time had the screens warned her that towering mountains were ahead. She swept clear of them with only a few feet to spare.

After that she encountered few obstacles and finally brought the machine down on what appeared to be a plain of highly glazed rock. The mist was still present, though not so dense as at the upper heights. The exterior searchlight projected perhaps a dozen yards, and the view, except for the color of the mist, looked exactly like some deserted quarter of London in the midst of a November night fog.

The Amazon said: "I'm willing to risk it in a space-suit outside if you are."

"I'm willing, but where's the point of it? Uranus is a pretty big planet, and if Viona is on it—which I greatly doubt—I don't see how we are to find her."

"We'll take portable radio and atmosphere-resonators. They will give a signal to show where we are even if Viona is unable to answer us."

Abna nodded, and they put on rubber and metal spacesuits as being the best protection against the planet's corrosive atmosphere.

The Amazon unfastened the inner airlock. Abna followed her, carrying the necessary instruments, closing the inner lock behind him, but leaving the lights on in the control room as a guide.

Moving back the clamps of the outer lock, the Amazon pulled back the heavy door, then she and Abna were exposed to the relentless atmosphere of Uranus, the acid dampness of it mottling their suits immediately and pitting tiny erosions on the glass of their helmet vizors.

The Amazon took several of the instruments Abna handed her, and then stepped outside to the slippery rock. It was of a curious composition, certainly unlike anything known on Earth, and it also seemed incapable of erosion, since it might have existed here ever since the planet had been born. Evidently Nature had created a form of ground-stuff that was resistant to the pitiless atmosphere.

"Any particular direction?" Abna asked, as the lights of the *Ultra* foundered in the mist behind and he kept on paying out the connecting lifeline through his gloved hands.

"How can there be?" the Amazon questioned, peering at the illuminated compass. "And, incidentally, this thing isn't working. Evidently Uranus' magnetic pole doesn't function as well as on other planets." She halted and then added: "We might try the radio again and see if there's any response."

Abna set the equipment down and looked at it anxiously. Its polished parts were already thick with defiling stains and the insulating material was smoking mysteriously.

"Let us try the atmosphere-resonators," the Amazon said.

She set down one of the instruments she was carrying. It was shaped rather like a small cannon, but it fired no shells. Instead it operated on the principle of vibrating sound-waves, transmitted by electric current from the self-contained generator.

When she pressed the main switch she and Abna heard, through their audiophones, the reverberating signal set up in the airwaves, which would travel to all parts of the planet without loss of strength. If Viona were alive on the planet she could not help but hear and understand.

"Now we've done that, what happens?" Abna asked, as they moved on again. "Depending on whereabouts Viona is on this terrible world, it may take her some time to reach us, and if by any chance her machine is wrecked she may never do so."

The Amazon seemed about to answer and then

paused, ducking quickly. Abna saw that something like the branch of a tree had flown past her head. A moment afterwards another object came drifting past on the poisonous air. It was like a ball with spiky protuberances all around it. It also possessed suckers, and it fastened on to the Amazon's spacesuit.

She hammered at it with her torch and it released its grip and drifted away.

"Life!" Abna exclaimed, startled. "And the most amazing life! Do you know what that thing was, Vi?"

"Of course I do—and the object before it. They're bacteria, enlarged to colossal size, the lowliest and yet the most indestructible form of life ever known. Bacteria on a giant scale is the only type of life which could live on a world like this."

"And inimical to us, judging from the attack."

The Amazon began moving on again. And Uranus had still more surprises to offer, for at length the rocky plain gave way to a jungle made up entirely of acid crystals—magnificent plants that looked like cut glass.

They reflected the light of the torches and some of them climbed up to 200 feet and more where they foundered in the mist. At intervals the weird bacterial life drifted among them, and every living shape was different, and every one as horrifying in appearance.

"Time we went back," the Amazon said at length. "We can fire another atmosphere-resonator from the *Ultra* to give our direction and then stay as long as we dare. The *Ultra*'s plates may get eaten through if we delay too long, and our suits are not going to last much longer either."

Then Abna found the lifeline was slack in his hands. He began hauling it in urgently, hoping he was merely taking up a loop—but finally he brought into view an end which had been bitten through, possibly through lying in an acid pool.

"The lifeline's snapped," he said. "We've no idea where the *Ultra* is. What about the compass tuned to her magnetic prow?"

The Amazon unhooked it from her belt and studied it carefully, but the needle was swinging idly with no fixed attraction.

CHAPTER SIXTEEN
REUNION IN SPACE

They turned and stumbled back the way they had come, by now utterly lost in the Uranian wilderness. Only once before had the Amazon ever been in a similar condition, and that had been on Venus—but here the danger was much more serious because of the atmosphere.

Bacteria flew swiftly over their heads—rods, bars and balls, equipped with deadly suckers and seeming to have no organized shape. Yet they did not pause to attack, a fact of which the Amazon presently came to take note.

"There must be something else somewhere of much more interest to them," Abna said, as the Amazon brought the matter to his notice.

"Obviously—but what? All forms of life—even bacteria—have their own hunting grounds, so why this sudden skirmish on their part? Only because of something new which is attracting them. I wonder if it's the *Ultra*?"

"It's got to be! Follow them—it's our only chance!"

This did not prove particularly difficult, for the

bacteria were present in ever-thickening hordes. All Abna and the Amazon had to do was stagger along across the saturating, rocky waste, filled now with the desperate hope that they might reach safety in time. Already the outer rubber coating of their space suits was commencing to peel away, exposing the first layer of metal mesh beneath.

Then they began to hear a strange sound. It resembled the rubbing of two sheets of sandpaper together and to it was added a queer chattering note. The cause of it seemed to be a dim, lighted blur commencing to take shape out of the fantastic mist.

"It's the *Ultra!*" Abna cried suddenly in immense relief, as he recognized the blur as an observation window with interior light streaming through it. "The noise is caused by those infernal bacteria rubbing against each other and talking in their own equivalent of a language."

Around the waiting ship were tens of thousands of bacteria crawling around the plates, jostling each other. And when they became aware of the approach of Abna and the Amazon, they swung around in their massed hordes and attacked.

Uncertain as to what might happen in such an atmosphere if they used their flame-guns, the Amazon relied on thrashing her way through the dense hordes with a small axe and the butt of her heavy proton gun. Abna used his mighty hands, encased in gloves, smashing the ferocious, nightmare life forms out of the way. Running the gauntlet to the airlock of the *Ultra* was something he and the Amazon would never be able to forget, but at last they were inside the inner lock and slammed the outer door. Dazed, they stumbled into the control room and pulled away their decaying suits.

Abna said: "I don't think Viona can be here. We had better return to Earth. As we go we can try and make contact with her by radio. She may know from Earth's broadcasts that things are back to normal, and in that case she'd surely return there. As for the Dark—well, unless we find Viona and Sefian, there's nothing we can do about it, except make preparations to die in a few years."

The Amazon said: "We are not going to die, Abna. We'll return to Earth, and if we cannot locate Viona we'll spend the next few years working on theory after theory to defeat the Dark."

She moved the control switches and the *Ultra* lifted into the mist.

She glanced back toward Neptune and Pluto—and then her gaze became fixed. Then she reached to the telescopic lens control and peered through it. Then she gave an exclamation of joy.

"Viona!"

Abna went over to her. Out in space, without the telescopic lens, he could see a dim silvery speck catching the light of the far distant sun, then as the Amazon sat aside he peered through the eyepiece intently. There was no doubt about it. There was a vessel out there, between Uranus and Neptune, and moving towards the outer planet at a comparatively leisurely speed.

"Thank heaven," Abna muttered, and it seemed a remarkably human exclamation from such a man as he. "It's her vessel. I can't understand why we missed her."

"I can," the Arnazon said, busy with the radio. "She must have flown away from Uranus' farther side just about the time we landed. Possibly our radio communication never reached her because of the magnetic disturbances which seem to exist on Uranus. Remember how they stopped the compasses operating?"

She switched on and spoke deliberately. With her free hand she was altering the *Ultra*'s course and turning it in the general direction of Neptune.

"Viona! Viona, come in. Your mother speaking."

An answer came, and on the scanning plate Viona's face appeared.

"Hello, mother!" she responded. "Where are you? I'm trying to spot you through the tele-reflector."

"Half a million miles from Uranus and following you. Your father and I have been through a ghastly experience trying to locate you."

"On Uranus, do you mean? It's not a nice planet, but it certainly has many fascinating secrets."

"Has it?" The Amazon looked surprised for a moment; then she came back to the business on hand. "Where are you heading for now?"

"Neptune. It's a long story explaining why, but I—"

"There's something more important on hand than visiting Neptune," the Amazon interrupted. "Stop your machine and we'll catch up with you.... I suppose

Sefian is still with you?"

"Yes, and in fine spirits. I'm sure I made the best decision leaving Earth as I did."

"We'll catch you," the Amazon said, and switched off.

The *Ultra* made short work of the millions of intervening miles—until at length both machines were level, and the vacuum-trap, an enclosed tunnel magnetically sealed from one vessel's airlock to the other, was put into place, and Viona came into the *Ultra*'s control room, carrying Sefian in her arms.

Abna took the child and set him down on the wall couch, where he began to play unconcernedly with the upholstery, while Viona gave her mother a hug.

"Why so solemn, mother?" she asked, seeing the Amazon's serious expression. "I thought you didn't mind me going off on my own to explore—after the way Sefner behaved."

"I didn't mind in the least. It's something more than that."

"Oh?" Viona turned away from Abna's massive embrace.

"First," the Amazon said, "you are a widow. Sefner Quorne is dead, killed by Kron of Zanji."

Viona shrugged. "We had reached the breaking point anyway," she said. "But you surely didn't chase all the way to Uranus to tell me that?"

"No; there was another reason. But first things first.... Everything is normal again on Earth now and the Zanjians have been wiped out. If no more invasions come from planets being overwhelmed by the Dark, Earth can settle down for a few years, until ultimate catastrophe."

"Just why didn't you answer our radio calls?" Abna asked.

"When I arrived on Uranus all radio contact became impossible. It is queerly magnetic—as perhaps you discovered?"

"We did," the Amazon assented.

"Yet full of mysterious remains from a marvellous civilization," Viona said. "I found a record in stone, un-eroded by acid, of an amazing race. You won't believe it, but they are educated, highly intelligent bacteria."

The Amazon smiled grimly. "Your father and I were nearly overwhelmed by them!"

"But you couldn't have been." Viona paused for a moment, puzzled. "They've left Uranus and gone to Neptune to establish a fresh civilization on a less unpleasant planet. The record I found in stone indicated as much by signs and symbols. It showed Neptune as the eighth world from the luminary. I was just on my way to Neptune when you contacted me."

Abna said: "There must be two types of bacterial life. You contacted the records of one form, Viona, and we contacted the remaining creatures—if you can call them such—still in actual existence."

"Bacterial life evolved to a high degree," the Amazon mused. "That is a wonderful thought. Bacterial life will, eventually, be the only form of life on Earth. That is, if life is not overwhelmed by the Dark. Bacterial life is the toughest, most resistant of all forms. I am wondering, since it can also have the power of intelligence, how mighty a civilization it may not have built for itself on Neptune."

"That," Abna said, "is hardly the point at issue."

The Amazon looked at Viona and then said deliberately, "Sefian, Viona, is the greatest genius that has ever been given to the System."

The girl smiled. "I am quite prepared to admit that he will be reasonably clever when he matures—which will be with considerable rapidity—but I'm afraid you are overestimating him, mother."

"No. He is a genius because he is no longer the child you brought into being. Even his individuality is not his own—or at least it will become increasingly less so—because he is little more than a reincarnation of Tarnec Brodix!"

"What!" Viona stared in amazement. "But—but how can he be?"

The Amazon gave the facts in detail, from the moment when she and Abna had entered the Dark. By the time she had finished there was a curious mixture of amazement and dismay on Viona's features.

"What right had Brodix to do such a thing?" she demanded.

"I suppose," Abna murmured, "one should feel flattered that of all the minds Brodix tested, only Sefian's proved worthy of receiving his information. But I can imagine how you feel. Your own child has in a sense been taken from you, and turned into—"

"A monster!" Viona declared flatly. "That's the only answer, father."

"Then it doesn't mean anything to you that your son can save the Universe?" the Amazon asked.

"No!"

Abna motioned to the meal he had laid out. "Perhaps we'd better eat," he suggested.

CHAPTER SEVENTEEN
TWO-YEAR-OLD GENIUS

During the meal, eaten leisurely, neither the Amazon nor Abna prompted Viona again. For most of the time she was silent, young Sefian eating at her side with all the composure of an adult.

"What—what would he have to do?" Viona asked at last, obvious fear in her blue eyes.

"I have no idea," the Amazon replied. "Brodix did not say. I imagine that we must talk to Sefian until his mind is able to grasp the deeper powers lying within it—as happened on the occasion when he released you from the Twenty-Fifth Plane—and then he will decide for himself what he must do. As I see it, the situation will be out of our control once he knows what he has to do."

"I might lose him," Viona pointed out. "I couldn't bear that."

The Amazon said: "The Dark will be upon us in three years or so, and that will be the end of everything. Sefian can save the Universe or he can die with the rest of us."

Viona gave her a look, glanced at Sefian, still busy

with his meal, and then walked to the window and looked out on the deeps of space.

"Why are you so concerned, mother?" Sefian asked calmly. "You know perfectly well that you will give in finally. It might just as well be now."

Viona swung and looked at him half in horror.

"I see again that strange change coming over him," Abna said. "The way he looked when he released us from the Twenty-Fifth Plane."

To have a two-year-old child talking with such perfect maturity, and eating a meal as any trained adult would, was uncanny enough—but so was the ring in his voice and the light of command in his violet eyes. His face was a puzzling cross-section of the Amazon, Sefner Quorne, and Viona herself, and there were glimpses of Abna, too.

"You have understood all we have been saying?" Viona asked in amazement. "All that your grand-mother said?"

"All the Golden Amazon said," Sefian corrected. "I prefer to give her her famous title than to call her grandmother. She is a product of science, as much as I am."

Sefian got down from his chair to the floor and stood thinking. It was a most amazing sight. A mere wisp of a child plunged into profound concentration. The very effort added tens of years to his otherwise unlined little face.

"The mention of the Dark provided the mental stim-ulus." he said. "And please do not look so surprised, mother! After all, I have the mind of Tarnec Brodix, or at least most of it, so how can I be just a child?"

Sefian climbed on to the seat under the observation window and looked out into space. He was silent for a long time, grappling with the immensity of the problem before him; then finally he said slowly:

"Yes, I can defeat it!"

"Defeat the Dark?" the Amazon asked quickly.

"Certainly. I have but to travel into the Dark, concentrate on the rearrangement of the variants, which caused the Fault to start, and inevitable mathematics will again rule the situation. At that moment the Dark will vanish as the error is removed and Brodix, too, will be recreated in his original form. That is a perfectly natural consequence because he is a part of the original sum."

"Did you say travel into the Dark?" Viona asked.

"I did. There is no other way."

"Because you must be part of the Fault in order to eliminate it?" she questioned.

"Exactly so."

"And what happens when Tarnec Brodix assumes his own personality again?" Abna asked. "As I see it, Sefian, all knowledge will be stripped from you as it returns to him, leaving you a child again, without knowledge, without the means to protect yourself."

"That," Sefian agreed, "will be the case."

Viona looked desperately from the Amazon to Abna, then at Sefian again.

"You can wear a space suit," the Amazon said. "That

will protect you when you revert to your natural self."

Sefian shook his head. "No, Golden Amazon, if I am to become a part of the Dark—as I must be to defeat it—I cannot wear a space suit. I cannot wear any clothes at all."

"But you'll die!" the Amazon exclaimed. "At least you will unless you adapt yourself beforehand to the conditions."

"In my case, Golden Amazon, that will not be necessary. I shall be a part of the Dark, and therefore sustained by it until the moment when I cancel the fault. After that I...."

"You will cease to exist!" Viona cried.

"Perhaps," Sefian responded, musing. "One can live in a void for a brief while since the void acts as a vacuum and seals in the bodily warmth. The only drawback will be the lack of air—"

"How far into the Dark would you have to go?" the Amazon asked.

"To its approximate center—which at the speed it is moving will take considerable calculation."

The Amazon said: "We can take Sefian as far as the edge of the Dark and—"

"You will not take me anywhere," Sefian interrupted. "I shall go alone. I wish to concentrate during the journey. I shall use the space machine you have out there, mother."

"But, Sefian—" Viona grasped his tiny shoulders tightly. "Sefian, what you are doing is gambling with death. To me, no Universe is worth that! Surely there is some other way in which you can—"

"There is no other way, and I cannot be dissuaded. I am speaking with the knowledge of Tarnec Brodix, not Sefian Quorne, and in that capacity am not touched by any human relationship."

"Would you have any objections if we followed in the *Ultra*?" the Amazon asked.

"None. But what have you in mind?"

"I was thinking that when the Fault is eliminated, we may be able to find your ship in the void and rescue you."

"I shall not be anywhere near my ship, Golden Amazon. In fact, I cannot give any guarantee where I shall be. Once I have flung myself into the Dark from the ship, by means of a spring ejector, I might drift anywhere the mathematical currents carry me."

Viona snapped: "He is not going to do it, not if I have to chain him down to stop him."

Sefian said: "You will not chain me down, mother, because I will not let you."

Viona made a grab at the child's wrists—but she did not continue to hold them. He looked at her so fixedly that she slowly straightened up again and backed away.

"I am sorry, mother," Sefian said quietly. "I have a task to do and I must do it. Now."

He turned to the airlock without another word, opened it, and then closed it behind him. Presumably he went through the vacuum trap to his own machine—or at least his mother's—for presently the trap was cast off from the vessel lying alongside the *Ultra* and it began to move.

"He even understood the switchboard," Viona whispered. "A child of two."

The Amazon settled at the control panels, withdrew the vacuum-trap, and then started the great machine forward in pursuit of Sefian's already speedily departing ship. To gradually narrow the distance was not very difficult despite the strain it threw on the Amazon, Abna and Viona as they watched fixedly through the window—but all their efforts were to no avail for, mysteriously, Sefian's machine vanished gradually before their eyes, leaving the void empty. Not far distant was Neptune, Pluto behind him, and behind them again the advancing wedge of the Dark.

"Where has he gone?" Viona asked in wonder. "He simply—dissolved!"

"Four-dimensional processes, I imagine," the Amazon responded. "The distance to the Dark is so enormous—even though it does not appear so from this position—it would take several lifetimes to reach it by ordinary methods. Sefian will have done as I did before—made a four-dimensional leap, so I will do the same."

She activated the controls and as on previous occasions the *Ultra* was rotated out of normal space and emerged again after a period of apparently flying through a region where the stars were crazily elongated. But the emergence from the leap through hyperspace did not reveal Sefian's machine, even though the solar system was now infinitely far away and the Dark much nearer. Evidently he was literally 'one jump ahead'.

It was not until at least eighteen 'jumps' had been made that his ship became visible again, a remote speck floating in front of the Dark.

The Amazon gradually swung the *Ultra* round so that it moved no nearer to the advancing tide.

"We'll wait and see what happens," she said, as Abna glanced at her. "If Sefian keeps his word, the Dark will lift and then we'll see if we can find him."

"We never shall," Viona whispered, swinging round with tears wet on her lashes. "I know we shan't! He's gone forever, and neither of you did any thing to try and stop it."

"Since you are overwrought," the Amazon responded, "we can overlook the unfairness of that comment. There was nothing we could do. A mind as powerful as Brodix can hold all of us in thrall—and you know it."

Meantime Sefian himself, a mighty mind in the body of a child, was alone in the Dark—but he interpreted it a very different way to that of the Amazon and Abna. To him the Dark was what Eddington had once called 'primal Universe stuff', the unformed material out of which Universes, by mathematics, are created. For him there was no sense of paralysis, since his mind was greater than the material conditions around him.

He was, nevertheless, in complete blackness, but the fact did not deter him in the least. From normal standards he was not breathing or living at all as a normal person should, existing only because his mind, or at least the mind which had been wished on him, was ruling the situation. He undressed calmly and then opened the outer airlock by finding his way to it. Feeling around for the ejector mechanism, he climbed into the firing tube and then pressed the automatic control. Immediately he was shot away from the vessel and out into the incomprehensible Dark

"I think," Abna said, when an hour of waiting had gone past, "that we had better take it in turns to watch. We have no idea how long Sefian may take—"

In the midst of his sentence the colossal Dark, which was devouring the infinite, suddenly ran into itself in the most amazing fashion. It looked like spilled ink photographed backwards so that the spill receded to a vanishing point and was gone. The stars blazed forth with their accustomed bewildering glory; the nebulae returned as the conditions normal to the Universe were re-established.

"He—he did it!" Abna whispered, hardly able to realize it. "He's destroyed the Dark!"

"Then—then where is he?" Viona demanded, working the telescopic lenses with desperate excitement. "Quick, mother—get the ship moving."

"I am already doing so," the Amazon answered, her voice quiet, and her violet eyes searched the canyons of infinity for some sign of a vessel. To detect a body so small as Sefian's she knew would be impossible.

She kept the *Ultra* moving, building speed upon speed until a velocity had been achieved which was the limit even she could take. It forced Viona full-length on to a wall couch and Abna braced his massive legs against the strain. To attempt the journey four-dimensionally was not practicable, for they might overshoot their goal—only vaguely known—and have to retrace.

After two hours of acceleration, in which time the *Ultra* fled through stupendous distances, the Universe seemed very little different in relation to the fixed stars, and there was certainly still no sign of Sefian or his machine.

"We've lost him," Viona declared. "Just as I knew we would."

The Amazon began speaking and then checked herself, studying something not far from the control panel. It seemed to be hanging in mid-air with all the indeterminacy of a ghost; then gradually it took definite shape. A familiar figure was standing in the *Ultra*—a small man in an abbreviated costume, his huge brain case supported by a curious cage-like affair joined to a collar that rested on his atrophied shoulders.

"Brodix!" Abna gasped, staring at him. The Amazon nodded slowly; then Viona got up from the wall couch and came striding forward angrily to the amazing entity.

"What are you doing here?" she demanded. "Where is my son, who made your return to life possible?"

"I am your son," the being answered calmly.

There was a stupefied silence. Viona's blue eyes opened wide and her mouth gaped for a moment.

"You?" she repeated. "What do you mean?"

"You are Tarnec Brodix," the Amazon said. "We

recognize you again."

"It would be more correct, Amazon, to say that I resemble Brodix—as indeed any creature must if he has reached the limit of evolution, as I have."

"The limit?" All Viona seemed capable of was repetition. "But if you are Sefian, you are a child and—"

"Sefian the child has gone forever," the creature replied. "In the few brief seconds while I mastered the infinite and reassembled the equations which had started the Fault and destroyed Tarnec Brodix, I evolved completely to the limit, and there I must remain. There is no such thing as de-evolution. Always forward, or else destruction."

"And Brodix himself? Did he not reassemble as he hoped?" Abna asked.

"No." The entity that had been a child brooded for a moment. "No—and I think the reason is not far to seek. When he transferred his knowledge to me, he did not transfer all of it—only part. Something was left out. Therefore, he could not reform, because I found it impossible to recreate the full total as far as he was concerned. Brodix and his mathematical planet existing beyond this Universe has gone forever. I remain—very much like him, but at heart I am still Sefian Quorne. I have, however, lost all humanity and am simply a mind with a physical vestment that obeys that mind. For that reason I am no longer one of you."

Viona backed away too appalled to speak, her eyes chained to the creature, who had once been her child.

"You will not work with us, beside us, to solve the

ultimate mysteries of the Universe?" the Amazon questioned.

It seemed that something like a smile quirked Seflan's thin-lipped mouth.

"To me there are no mysteries left, Amazon. I must go to greater things, out beyond the next Universe, beyond that again—outward, into the Ultimate."

There was silence, then Sefian made a final statement: "You will never see me again, nor will you ever hear of Tarnec Brodix, who has ceased to exist. Whatever problems you may face you will solve for yourselves. You...." Sefian's tiny eyes switched to Viona's blank face. "You gave to the Universe a being who saved it. Be grateful for that, if for nothing else."

Then, abruptly, Sefian was gone. The control room was as empty as though he had never been. Viona sat for a few moments staring straight in front of her, then getting suddenly to her feet she went to her private chamber.

Abna said moodily: "She's young and much more a human being than you or I. We might brush away such a thing but she can't. Unless—"

The Amazon glanced up from the instruments. "Yes?"

"Unless I use my mental powers to destroy the ache in her heart and mind. As a father I suppose I should."

Abna did not explain any further. He turned and went along the passage to Viona's room. Knocking on the door, he went inside. He seated himself on the edge of the small bed on which Viona was lying. She had not put on the light, but the glow of the stars shone on her pale face.

"What is it, father?" she asked quietly. "I don't want to sound hurtful, but I'd much sooner be left alone."

Abna did not answer. Instead he leaned a little closer so that he could see Viona's eyes clearly. In this light they looked black. She looked back into his and, after a moment, tried to look away—but was unable. A growing drowsiness was stealing over her—a sense of peace and well being, and very gradually it dissolved into deep sleep. Abna smiled, patted her shoulder gently, and then got to his feet. He stood for a moment looking through the porthole toward the stars, then he turned and left. The Amazon glanced at him inquiringly as he came into the control room again.

"Viona will be Viona again when she awakens," he said.

"What did you do?"

"I blotted out the memory of everything which has happened to her since she became the wife of Sefner Quorne. That is going back some distance, I know, and takes a pretty large slice out of her life—but it is surely better that way? Many more people would be happier and live longer if they had the power of obliterating memory. Naturally there will be many things she will not be able to understand or piece together—but the names of Quorne or Sefian, or mention of the departed Dark will mean nothing to her."

The Amazon smiled a little. "It is fortunate, Abna, that your godlike powers are only used on rare occasions and for beneficent reasons. I am afraid that if I were able to rise to such heights I— But I'm not able," she broke off, shrugging. "And perhaps it's just as well."

CHAPTER EIGHTEEN
STRANGE NEW WORLD

It was six hours later, and the *Ultra* was within telescopic sight of the Solar System once more, when Viona came into the control room. The Amazon and Abna were having a meal together when she arrived, the machine flying onward at a constant velocity through free space.

"So I am aboard the *Ultra*!" Viona said, looking about her as she came in. "Funny thing is I can't remember how I got here.... Ah, a meal!" she broke off, her eyes brightening. "Just what I can do with."

Abna pushed over the dish of concentrates and studied the girl casually for a moment. She glanced through the observation window and asked: "Where are we?"

"Three hundred and twenty million miles from the orbit of Pluto," the Amazon answered.

Viona ate in silence for a while and then drank some restorative. Finally she said: "I suppose a young person like I am can't really suffer from amnesia, yet I do believe that is what has happened. I clearly remember talking to Mr. Wilson aboard a space liner and then—

well, now I'm here. It doesn't make sense at all."

The Amazon gave Abna a sharp glance. He had evidently taken the girl back a tremendous way in memory, to a time before she had even seen Sefner Quorne. In fact, several years had dropped into oblivion.

"Chris Wilson told us what happened," Abna said. "After you left him, you were struck by a chunk of meteoric iron and it caused a brain injury. The best cure seemed to be to take you into space for a complete rest—so here you are."

Viona did not say anything, but her blue eyes pinned her father's steadily. He smiled rather uncomfortably under the scrutiny.

"A man of your powers, father, does not need to talk about brain injuries and rest in space," Viona said at last. "You can cure injuries on the spot."

"In this case I was not around to do so at the time. The fact remains we brought you into space to recuperate—and apparently you have done so."

There was a long, hesitant moment while it seemed that Viona would start questioning all over again; then apparently she resigned herself to the enigmatic situation for she gave a bright smile.

"Well, I feel healthy enough anyway, so what happens next?"

"We have been touring space with no particular objective," the Amazon answered, "but we had thought of visiting Neptune on our way home. It's a planet that might bear inspection. During our outward trip, your father and I had a look at Uranus and, while there, found records concerning a bacterial race of high intelligence, which migrated to Neptune many generations ago. A race like that might be worth contacting."

"Might indeed," Viona agreed. "Liven the monotony anyway."

Abna glanced at the Amazon. It was perfectly clear now that no hint of memory remained in Viona's mind. She went on with her meal and waited for the next.

"We shall reach Neptune in about six hours at our present velocity," the Amazon announced, glancing toward the instruments. "Until then I think we might as well take it in turns to rest."

Six hours later the *Ultra* touched the outermost edge of Neptune's atmospheric envelope, and began to move downward. Viona had taken over Abna's customary job of checking the exterior conditions and presently she looked up in some bewilderment.

"There is something very strange, here," she said. "By all normal standards, a planet this far from the sun ought to be frozen, but it isn't. The exterior thermometer registers eighty degrees Fahrenheit. About the same as a comfortable Earth summer day."

"Decidedly strange," the Amazon agreed, puzzled. "What is the atmosphere content? To be normal, it should be either ammoniated hydrogen or nitric acid gas."

"It is neither," Viona said, studying the gauge. "It's oxygen, hydrogen, krypton, argon— In fact, the identical ingredients to those of Earth."

The Amazon frowned all the more deeply, and so did Abna. As scientists they both knew—as indeed did Viona—how utterly incredible it was that a planet on the rim of the Solar System should have all these gases and a normal temperature. The mystery was deepened by the atmosphere being green, which did not fit in at all with the gases Viona had named.

"Colour wavelength very predominant," she said, which immediately gave the explanation. "The green wavelength takes precedence over all others and is caused by water vapour refraction."

The Amazon did not say anything. Her curiosity was sharply aroused. She kept on guiding the *Ultra* downward with ever-decreasing speed, until at last the great vessel came below the blanketing mists of the upper heights, and here indeed the mystery assumed incredible proportions.

The view below was identical to that of Earth! There were oceans, landscapes, cities, and mountains—the entire topography, and almost in exactly the same scale as on Earth's surface.

"What in cosmos are we looking at?" the Amazon demanded blankly, giving a glance at the astounded faces of Abna and Viona. "This is Earth, and the surface light is almost the same too, despite the distance from the sun...."

"That could be done by light-wave trapping," Abna said quickly. "Obtaining solar light-photons in their original power and then reflecting them. The process is not unknown to higher scientific thought. But...."

He stopped, faced by a riddle he could not understand. The Amazon said nothing for a while as she
continued driving the vessel downward. She headed in
the direction of 'London' because it seemed the only
logical thing to do.

"I wonder," the Amazon said, "if Earth and Neptune
have somehow changed places?" Then she shook her
head impatiently at such a thought. "No, that isn't it.
This is definitely Neptune—the dimensions of the
landscape prove it."

"There are people down there," Viona said suddenly,
pointing. "Look!"

Her mother and father had already seen them. She
turned quickly to the telescopic mirror and adjusted it.
On to the screen flashed a picture of men and women
going to and fro on the great pedestrian tracks, people
dressed in the fashion prevailing on Earth. And on
the traffic levels were vehicles also conforming to the
Earth standards.

"It's beyond comprehension," the Amazon said,
turning the *Ultra*'s nose to a spaceport.

She brought the machine down safely and cut off the
power plant. Outside the vessel other machines were
lined up, all of the conventional design. The mechanics
tending them were entirely Earth-like in appearance,
and not paying much attention to the *Ultra*'s arrival.

"Gravity similar to Earth's as well," Viona said,
flexing her knees to prove it.

"That's understandable," Abna said. "Neptune is
not very densely packed despite its size, so the gravity

is about equal to Earth's own. I wish everything else could be explained as easily."

He moved to the airlock and opened it. Soft, warm air came sweeping into the control room; then standing aside for the Amazon and Viona to go before him, he followed them out to the hard stone of the runway.

"Better find out what we can," the Amazon said, and signalled to a mechanic. He came over, but there was no surprise on his features as he studied the three arrivals.

"Where are we?" the Amazon asked.

The man hesitated, puzzled. Then when he spoke it was in a babble of alien words that made no sense—except that "Maxicon" seemed to be repeated several times. The Amazon held up her hand and dismissed him.

"He doesn't speak English anyway," she said. "Better try and find somebody in authority."

She, Viona, and Abna started moving again, and indeed they were on quite familiar ground, for the exit to the spaceport was identical to what it was on Earth. They walked to the center of 'London', finding everything just where they expected to find it.

At length they came to the Space Line Executive Building. They went in and took the elevator, and the Amazon knocked on the door of Chris Wilson's office.

"Come in," requested the voice of Wilson, in English.

They walked in, and Chris Wilson—or at least somebody incredibly like him—was at the desk, but there was no light of recognition in his eyes.

"Something I can do for you?" he inquired pleasantly.

"Do for us?" the Amazon repeated, her face blank. "Chris, what sort of a game is this? Surely you know us?"

"I'm afraid I don't. Should I?" He motioned them to be seated.

"Just who are you?" the Amazon asked, her eyes pinning him.

"The name is Wilson—Christopher Wilson. I am the chief executive of the Space Line."

"But that operates from Earth!" Viona put in, amazed. "This is Neptune, Mr. Wilson!"

"Neptune?" Chris looked vague for a moment. "Oh, you mean this world? It is called Maxicon, not Earth."

"Whatever it is called," Abna said deliberately, "it exactly duplicates Earth, the third world from the sun, in every detail."

"So it should," Chris responded. "We went to a great deal of trouble to get that effect, even to learning all known languages."

"A mechanic at the spaceport did not talk English," Viona pointed out.

"Possibly not. Some haven't yet overcome the language difficulty. He probably used his own tongue."

The Amazon suddenly banged her fist on the desk. "Is there any reason why I can't know what all this is about?" she demanded. "Why is Maxicon a duplicate of Earth?"

"The people of the third world," Chris answered,

"are quite unharmed, and so are the buildings around them. We are beneficent scientists, not destroyers."

The Amazon hesitated, aware of the problem with which she was grappling. Then she asked: "Are the people on this world duplicates of Earth people in every sense of the word?"

"They are: and the originals are not aware of it. Somewhere on this planet, if you three are Earth people, there will be duplicates of you, too."

"Have you the authority to explain everything?" Abna questioned.

"No, but I can have you taken to the head of the state. I don't doubt he will gladly explain."

'Chris Wilson' pressed a button on his desk and a clerk came in.

"Be good enough to take these ladies and the gentleman to Dral," the duplicate Chris requested. "They wish an audience with him."

The clerk nodded, and then led the way from the room. The trio followed him to the roof and a helico-plane. The clerk was evidently a pilot as well, and in a few minutes he brought the trio down on the flat roof of the building where the government was housed, exactly as it was in London. As she stepped out of the cabin doorway, the Amazon looked at the sky. It was pale green.

The clerk led them to the office of the head of the state.

"Please be seated," he requested gravely.

CHAPTER NINETEEN
THE EARTH IN DUPLICATE

The three obeyed, and the Amazon asked for an explanation. In response, Dral gave his serious smile.

"Naturally the condition is puzzling to you, but it is mainly the outcome of necessity. Some time ago we were bacterial life—or you would call it such—and though we had almost indestructible powers, we were nevertheless handicapped by lack of useful physical form. We came originally from the seventh planet from the luminary, leaving that world because it had nothing to offer us with its poor quality atmosphere. We propelled ourselves here through space, the void making no difference to our type of bodies as they were then. Then we held a meeting to decide what must be done. We have the mastery of mental processes, but found ourselves handicapped by lacking physical form with which to work. So we decided on duplication. A bacterial body is basically a parasite and because of that is capable of forming into any shape. But we needed a pattern to which we could all conform. So, knowing from spatial excursions we had made—as bacteria, of course—that Earth people possessed the most versatile bodies, we decided to duplicate ourselves like them."

"How?" Abna questioned.

"Having the mastery of mental processes, all we needed to do was place ourselves in sympathy with the mental vibration of the person we selected, and so our bacterial-shaped body conformed to the mental pattern received."

"You mean the mental vibrations of the person you selected travelled this far?" the Amazon asked. "To this outpost of the System?"

"Certainly. Thought waves are the one form of radiation that do not lose strength as distance increases. So, since there were as many of us as there are people on Earth, we were all amply suited—able to make our choice as to which body we would take. There are still some thousands of our original bacteria-shaped race left without a vestment, but their turn will come as Earth's population increases."

"And you have even chosen the same names!" Viona exclaimed. "Christopher Wilson, for one, who sent us here."

"That is a purely optional point," Dral replied. "Some of us retain our own names—as I have—and others assume the name of the person whom they have used as a pattern. However, once we had taken over physical images, the rest was simple. We built cities identical to those used by our pattern people, and forced the topography of this world to conform to that of the third. Why? Because, obviously the physique of a third-world person which we have taken requires a third-world environment. Here you will find, I think, every person you have ever known—duplicated."

"In that case," the Amazon said, "I assume we three here are also duplicated?"

"Certainly. And those who have taken your patterns have also taken your names— The Golden Amazon, Viona, and Abna. Those names are correct, are they not?"

"Correct," Abna agreed.

"There is also," Dral added, "one called Sefner Quorne, who seems in some way to be connected with you—though when we took his pattern, he was apparently an enemy of yours. Naturally he is not an enemy in the duplicate form, as the original character is not repeated."

The Amazon gave Viona a sharp look as a puzzled expression came over her face. For just a moment it was plain her memory was groping backwards, trying to ascertain where Quorne ought to fit into her scheme of things. Before she could perhaps gain some latent gleam of the past, the Amazon spoke quickly.

"I assume, Dral, that the civilization you have duplicated here has the same aspirations as our own?"

"By no means. We are infinitely above you in our concepts. We use similar cities to aid our Earth-like physiques, as I told you. But our aims and purposes go right out into the Universe itself. That is why we shield our world with perpetual mist: that is why we never openly visit the world from which we have taken our pattern."

"Did your aims and purposes include—the Dark?" the Amazon questioned, and for a moment a puzzled look crossed Dral's face.

"If you refer to the tide of dissolution that was spreading over the face of the Universe, yes," he answered. "We were working on it when it disappeared. And we would like to know why it happened, and even more so why it vanished."

"Perhaps," Abna said vaguely, "a mathematician somewhere."

"A possibility," Dral replied.

The Amazon asked: "What happens if the pattern from which you are moulded dies? Does your image of it die, too?"

"No. Not any more than the offspring dies at the death of the parent."

"I think," the Amazon said, "we can do little now but pay you our interplanetary respects and continue our journey. We are bound for Earth and since chance brought us to Neptune, we—"

"Chance?" Dral asked quietly. "What chance?"

"Exploration of Uranus, the next planet to this one, led us to discover records of your race which had come here—so we came to look. Pure curiosity, of course."

"A dangerous curiosity, I'm afraid," Dral commented, getting to his feet. "I have already explained that our world is sheathed in green vapour so none can penetrate it—visually at least. Those who do it physically cannot be permitted to leave."

"What!" Abna cried, jumping up. "That's utterly

preposterous—and against the Interplanetary Code!"

"We do not acknowledge any Interplanetary Code," Dral replied. "We are a law unto ourselves. We are hospitable scientists, yes, but we are not fools. You have surely realized what would happen were you to continue on your way to Earth with the story of this world? Before long we would be overrun with people from Earth wishing to make contact with their doubles. Natural curiosity alone would cause that."

"And if we give our word not to mention a thing about this planet?" the Amazon asked.

"With all due deference, Amazon, your word would not be accepted. We of Maxicon know all about you— and we know you break your word whenever it happens to suit your requirements."

"But you can't mean we have to stop here indefinitely!" Viona cried.

"That is the ruling. You will be our guests. I will make immediate arrangements."

Dral pressed a switch on his desk and after a moment a servant in uniform entered. Dral gave his instructions.

"Our three interplanetary friends here will be guests for an indefinite period," he said. "Make every arrangement for their comfort in the guest residence."

The servant saluted and led the way from the room. Without further words to Dral, the trio went out, down the long corridor, and finally into other quarters of the great official building where there extended a suite of rooms magnificently furnished.

"You will find all you require here," the servant said. "Refreshments will be sent to you shortly."

He went out, and the door locked itself electrically.

Abna said: "These people seem to have all necessities for making their orders inescapable. Electric locks on the door—bars on the windows, which are probably electrically livened."

The Amazon looked toward the great floor-to-ceiling openings giving on to a metal balcony and view of the city. Bars were placed every few inches and each bar was two inches thick. Experimentally she took one of her instruments from her belt and threw it forward. The instant it hit the bar it vanished in a blinding flash of flame.

"You guessed right, father," Viona commented.

Abna did not seem to hear the girl. He went across to the bars, hesitated, then grasped one of them. He smiled a little.

"As I thought," he said. "You short-circuited the current, Vi. These bars are just plain metal at the moment. Doubtless our friends will have noticed the fault and will straighten it out, but until then we—"

He paused as the Amazon was on the point of removing her disintegrator gun from her belt. She put it back there, but kept her hand on it as the servant returned into the room. Before him he was directing a heavily loaded tray, which floated in mid-air on a magnetic beam. By a mere movement of his hand he brought the tray to rest on a table.

CHAPTER TWENTY
THE AMAZON COMES THROUGH

Silently the Amazon drew out her disintegrator, her face cruelly set. She fired, but no brief destructive beam came forth. The servant continued setting out the meal and presently turned. There was an odd gleam in his eye, almost a sinister amusement.

"With deference, Golden Amazon," he said, "I would remark that weapons are useless. The same waves that carried this tray are also passing through this room, neutralizing every other type of radiation—including guns. If there is anything further you wish, please ring."

The Amazon's fury, already at white heat, spilled over. Radiation might be blocked, but her muscles were not. She lashed out her right fist with devastating impact, sending the hapless servant flying against the wall. He hit it with such force the concussion stunned him, and he slid to the floor.

Hardly had he dropped than the Amazon swung to the door—but in the interval it had closed and locked itself and the electric fastening was beyond her power of breaking.

"The window," she said abruptly, hurrying to it. "If we can smash these bars aside.... Abna—Viona—give me a hand."

They hurried to assist her, knowing everything depended on speed. It was more than possible that the suite was wired with television-sound and that everything they said and did was being picked up somewhere in headquarters. With their united strength they seized the bars and pulled on them, but mighty though their combined strength was, they could not budge them.

Finally they desisted, breathing hard. Between the bars they could see the not far-distant spaceport and the lines of the *Ultra* among the other machines.

"Got to be some way," Abna breathed, clenching his fist. "If we could only get out of here, it's only a hop to the *Ultra* and we'd fight our way somehow—"

The door opened, and the Amazon's hand flew to her gun. Then she remembered, and her expression changed to surprise as she surveyed the three who entered. Apparently they were herself, Abna, and Viona. Identical in every detail except clothes. The trio did not close the door behind them; they came forward, as much wonder in their eyes as there was in the eyes of those from whom they were patterned.

"We came to see the three we chose as our models," Amazon II explained. "We are permitted to do that by the law. It is a most uncanny experience."

There were differences in the way this duplicate Amazon spoke. Her tone was softer and quieter—it had none of the bite peculiar to the Amazon herself.

"It is not the first time I have looked upon the image of myself," the Amazon answered briefly. "I have made synthetic models of myself before today. Tell me, is your strength similar to mine?"

Amazon II shook her head. "No. We take only the outer physical vestment. The muscular development is not reproduced, any more than is the actual nature."

"Which is all I wanted to know," the Amazon murmured. "Viona—get to that door and stop it shutting."

Viona hurled herself to it. It was already commencing to move gently to a close but just in time she rammed her foot between it and the frame.

"Thank you, my friend, for coming here," the Amazon continued dryly. "We were just looking for a means of escape and apparently we have found it—"

With that she hesitated no longer. Hurling herself at her double, she bore the frightened creature to the floor before she—or it—had the least chance to resist. Not that it would have been any use against the Amazon's steel muscles in any case. Abna was already dealing with his own twin who, though mighty in stature, was as weak as a baby in Abna's hands. Viona's double was simple to deal with. One blow from the Amazon's fist flattened her out helplessly on the floor.

In a matter of moments the outer clothes had been whipped from the backs of the helpless three and were adorning the originals, then the Amazon led the way out into the corridor and looked about her.

"We can risk it," she murmured. "Come!"

Abna and Viona followed her out, closing the door behind them. Whether the three imprisoned in their place knew how to control the electric lock from the inside was something they had to chance. Apparently they did not, for there was no immediate pursuit.

They went past the guard at the entrance to the building and he took no notice, evidently having seen 'them' come in. On the street they began to hurry once more—and three armed men suddenly appeared from a side street.

The Amazon did not stop to think how these men might be able to use their guns whereas hers would not work. In any case, it was too buried in her excess of clothing to be reached—so she plunged forward and hammered her fists into the guards' faces before they had a chance to draw. One reeled backward and collapsed. The second staggered, then fell over as Viona slammed home a killing blow to the stomach. The third man stood no chance against Abna. He whipped him high over his head and then flung him against a nearby building.

The incident showed that Dral knew what had transpired, so the trio hurled caution to the wind and hurried as rapidly as possible in the spaceport's direction.

It appeared that Dral had placed full reliance on the three guards he had dispatched, for there were no further attempts to stop their escape—until they reached the *Ultra* itself, then from inside it a man appeared, gun in hand. He was so obviously ready to fire it would have been dangerous to tackle him there and then.

But it was not this fact which prevented the Amazon, Abna, or Viona from acting: it was the realization that this guardian of the *Ultra* had heliotrope-colored eyes and dead black hair.

"Quorne!" the Amazon whispered

Then the guard spoke—and his voice was remarkably like Sefner Quorne's.

"I have taken the name of my original pattern because I like it," he said politely. "Sefner Quorne.... It has an impressive ring to it, don't you think? I am also head of the guard in Dral's headquarters. He dispatched me here to dissuade you from any intentions you might have regarding escape."

Quorne II glanced at Abna and then Viona, and in those split seconds while his attention was diverted, the Amazon lunged forward in a flying tackle, caught him around the knees, and overbalanced him. Then he was toppled helplessly over her shoulder, to crash to the ground, his gun flying out of his hand.

This was the only break the three needed. They tumbled through the open airlock into the ship, and slammed the door. While Viona moved the sealing sheath into place, the Amazon snapped on the power switches—to find no current was in action.

"That neutralizing power is still at work," she said bitterly, glancing over her shoulder. "I've only one chance—to use the degravitator emergency plates. They'll kill gravity under the vessel, but the strain will be terrific for us as well as the ship. Gravity isn't a force as such, so we may succeed."

With that she made the requisite connection. Instantly the *Ultra* began rising with demonical speed, no longer chained by gravity. Rarely did the Amazon use such desperate expedients because of the terrific stress involved, but this time there was no alternative.

Gasping with the pain in her nearly crushed lungs, she lay flat on the floor, brilliant lights bursting before her eyes. Nearby she saw the purpling faces of Viona and Abna as they too lay flattened on the plates, unable to raise themselves. Abna made a slight effort, but his position was such he could get no leverage.

The Amazon braced one forearm beneath her and felt as if it would crack under the weight of her body. Using every vestige of her supernormal strength, she dragged up her other arm and forced her hand higher and higher, until it came within reach of the degravitator switch. She pulled it and fell flat—and almost immediately she was floating from the floor, acceleration cut out.

Panting for breath, she clutched the switchboard and straightened up, helping Viona and Abna to rise beside her. They looked back toward Neptune.

"They're not following," Abna said at last. "I suppose they mean to let us get away with it. Not that I can see why they need to worry so much about their precious duplicate planet."

"They worry because of the secrets they possess which we might discover," the Amazon answered as she set the course for Earth. "And I am none too sure that we won't—someday."

Abna and Viona looked at her quickly. She gave a grim smile.

"Ask yourselves," she exclaimed, motioning back to the green world vanishing in the gulf. "A world which duplicates everything Earth possesses and which—according to Dral—has many things we have not. A higher order of science altogether. Do you really believe that those Earth duplicates are just behaving like Earth people because they require a physical vestment? No. It is something more than that."

"Perhaps," Abna said, "you are right."

"I am convinced of it. And what is more, I cannot believe that guard was only a duplicate of Sefner Quorne. His every action, his every word, was Sefner Quorne to the life. How could it be if the individuality of the man imitating him is different?"

The Amazon ceased talking. She was venturing into deep waters. Abna and Viona did not speak either. They were looking away toward the eighth planet as it receded into the maw of the everlasting stars.

ABOUT THE AUTHOR

British writer **JOHN RUSSELL FEARN** was born near Manchester, England, in 1908. As a child he devoured the science fiction of Wells and Verne, and was a voracious reader of the Boys' Story Papers. He was also fascinated by the cinema, and first broke into print in 1931 with a series of articles in *Film Weekly*.

He then quickly sold his first novel, *The Intelligence Gigantic*, to the American magazine, *Amazing Stories*. Over the next fifteen years, writing under several pseudonyms, Fearn became one of the most prolific contributors to all of the leading US science fiction pulps, including such legendary publications as *Astounding Stories*, *Startling Stories*, *Thrilling Wonder Stories*, and *Weird Tales*.

During the late 1940s he diversified into writing novels for the UK market, and also created his famous superwoman character, The Golden Amazon, for the prestigious Canadian magazine, the Toronto *Star Weekly*. In the early 1950s in the UK, his fifty-two novels as "Vargo Statten" were bestsellers, most notably his novelization of the film, *Creature from the Black Lagoon*.

Apart from science fiction, he had equal success with westerns, romances, and detective fiction, writing an amazing total of 180 novels—most of them in a period of just ten years—before his early death in 1960. His work has been translated into nine languages, and continues to be reprinted and read worldwide.